THE LAST FLOWER
By Narcissus Blue

This is a work of fiction. All characters and events in this book are from the author's imagination. Any resemblance to actual persons, living or dead, events, or locales is entirely coincidental.

The Last Flower Copyright © 2025 by
Narcissus Blue

All rights reserved.
No part of this book may be reproduced or used in any manner without written permission of the copyright owner except for the use of quotations in a book review.

CHAPTER ONE
Bryn

Earth was dying, gasping out its last breath as we abandoned it. Humans flee the irreversible damage they had done. We left it all behind. I left it all behind. Our once beautiful planet grows smaller the further we travel into space. There weren't many people left on Earth when I decided to leave. My family had passed away and I had no more ties keeping me there. The rich were the first to leave, taking the expensive ships and filling them with their family and friends. People like me, the rejects and the poor, were made to leave last. Our government left behind small escape pods with the coordinates to the new planet already set. We just had to press a button and it would take us there.

Each pod could accommodate six people. An officer quickly divided us up between the rest of the pods, and I ended up sharing one with five other females. I didn't miss the amused looks on their faces when I passed them on my way to my seat. People stared at me a lot. They either loved what they saw, or hated it. My skin was pale, the only trace of color that can be seen is if I blush or get sunburn. My mother always kept me inside, because my skin and eyes were so sensitive to the sun. The only time I could ever go out without sunglasses and a hat, was when it rained. I weakly smile, remembering those sweet days, playing in puddles and getting muddy.

I nervously twirled my white hair and fidgeted in my seat as the A.I gave instructions before we took off. I took a few steadying breaths after fastening my seat belts. The women on board chatted animatedly like it was a completely normal day. No one spoke to me and I was fine with that.

I was startled by the engine rumbling to life with a bone-deep vibration. A rising whine turned into a deafening roar as the thrusters engaged.

The A.I counted down from ten. "Ten, nine, eight."

My heart leapt into my throat and I squirmed in my seat. "Seven, six."

I gripped the armrests and squeezed my eyes shut. "Five, four, three, two, one."

A sudden, gut-wrenching force pressed me into the seat as the pod lurched free, hurtling skyward in a violent surge of fire and speed. I forced air through my nose and out my mouth as the pod soared through Earth's atmosphere. My heart stops when the pod suddenly floats for a few seconds mid-air. I stare out the window, panicked, until a second jolt sends me back into my seat. The back-up thrusters engaged. I wipe the sweat from my brow and close my eyes, willing this trip to go as fast as possible.

"Hey...I'm Mary."

At the sound of the meek voice, I open my eyes and find a woman staring at me with a gentle smile on her face. She was petite, with cool blue eyes and her dark locs were styled in a dramatic bob. She looks at me curiously and I realize I haven't said a word yet.

"I'm Bryn," I say with a friendly smile.

She shakes my hand and admits, "I've never seen eyes like yours. They're stunning."

"Thank you."

My eyes were a pale shade of purple, another trait of my condition. I was happy to hear that she liked them, most people I've met found them unnerving.

Mary leaned over the aisle, "I'm so excited to see the new planet. How about you?"

I was excited. I just hoped we could take care of this planet and not destroy it like the last. "I am excited."

Mary smiled and after a few awkward moments, she must have realized I wasn't going to talk much, and turned to another woman to chat. They were deep in conversation as I turned to look out the window. The stars looked like millions of scattered diamonds against the endless backdrop of space. The A.I played gentle music, and with the calming hum of the pod's hull, I quickly dozed off to sleep. But the peace was short-lived.

I woke up to the sound of panicked voices.

"Please fasten your seatbelts. Your pod has been disengaged and will head to the closest planet," the calm voice of the ships A.I announced through the speakers. Flurries of questions spilled from the other women.

"What the hell does that mean?"
"I knew this would happen."
"They disengaged the escape pod!"

I shot to my feet and faced a bigger woman, her face in a permanent frown, "Who disengaged it?"

"The government, the rich- take your pick!"

Another warning blared through the speakers, more urgent this time. "Fasten your seatbelts, we are entering the atmosphere."

A sudden bout of turbulence threw us together and we crashed to the floor of the pod with pained groans. We scrambled to our seats as fast as we could.
I swallowed my panic and stared out the window. The escape pod tore through the atmosphere and plummeted toward the ground like a dying star. The world came into view and from what I could see, it was a lot like Earth. That thought gave me a modicum of peace before it was left behind,

burned up in our blazing trail. The pod gave a final lurch, and then the thrusters cut off. Complete silence filled the space for a brief moment. Then we started to fall. The women around me screamed, and I stared wide eyed, watching the scene blur and pass us in a flurry of colors. *Where's the parachute?*

My breathing grew ragged the longer I waited for the chute to appear and save us from smashing into the unforgiving ground below. I closed my eyes and listened to Mary and the other girls cry. They cried for their mothers, and some cried to their gods. I gritted my teeth, bracing for impact. There was nothing we could do, except embrace what was coming. The sound of the parachute finally deploying gave me hope. Then my world went dark.

A gentle breeze tickled my sensitive flesh, the patter of cold raindrops made me shiver. My neck pinches when I try to raise my head. I slowly peek through my light lashes, struggling to open my eyes fully against the brightness of my surroundings.

"Is everyone okay?" I call to the other girls. Silence.

I move slowly to unbuckle myself, even though every muscle screams at me to stay still. I move my legs, stretching and rotating them, thankfully finding no injuries. I force my eyes open, and take in the sight before me. Plains, as far as the eye can see. The land was flat, with tall grass swaying in the silent breeze, carrying the scent of an impending thunderstorm. The sky was a pale shade of cyan, but dark clouds loomed just beyond a jagged mountain range in the distance. Overhead, strange birds soared, their silhouettes a haunting reminder that this was an unknown world. I stare in awe as twin moons emerge, growing brighter against the darkening sky.

The vivid greens blur as my gaze drifts downward, and that's when I see it. The wreckage. My breath catches in my throat as the realization hits, half of the pod is gone. Along with the girls. *Did we clip the mountain?* Panic gnaws at me, but then I glance to my left and feel a rush of relief. Mary's still in her seat, untouched. A weight lifts from my chest, but as I try to move, a sharp pain lances through my arm. I look down to find a long, jagged gash running along my forearm. I pull off my cardigan and wrap it tightly around the wound before pushing myself toward Mary.

"Mary… Mary?" She didn't wake, but she was alive, her chest rose and fell as she slept. I decided to let her sleep and moved back to my seat. Then I hugged my knees to my chest and finally let myself cry.

Mary didn't wake until the twin moons were high in the sky. "What are we going to do?"

I didn't know. I had already searched the pod and only found one water bottle and a flashlight. Everything else was gone. Luckily, everyone's luggage was kept in the back of the pod. I looked through them one by one, finding a few protein bars, a small first aid kit and a small pocket knife. I cleaned my wound the best I could. The alcohol wipes burned like hell. I gritted my teeth as I carefully cleaned the blood and dirt from my cut, then I used all the gauze to wrap it.

"We can't go anywhere tonight. We don't know what kind of animals are on this planet, it could be really dangerous."

Mary nodded her head. Thankfully, Mary wasn't hurt in the crash, just really sore. She barely moved from her spot. I passed her a protein bar and we both ate greedily. Afterwards, we laid together, trying to keep warm. The temperature dropped as night came and we shivered uncontrollably. I tried to get comfortable and closed my eyes, only to be woken up by Mary's urgent whispers.

"Did you hear that?"

I tensed and remained completely still. A loud jeer echoed in the distance, like a warning in the night.

"It sounds like a blue jay," I say, my voice unsteady as I grasp for something familiar, anything, to anchor us. Something that feels safe. I need it to feel safe. But Mary sees right through me.

"We're not on Earth anymore, Bryn."

No we weren't.

Just then, a loud bang shook the damaged pod. We scrambled back, until our backs were against the furthest wall, away from the torn opening. I inhale sharply when a silhouetted figure steps out of the shadows. Mary clutched my injured arm, and I cried softly. I gritted my teeth as pain shot through my arm, and I felt a fresh stream of blood seep from the wound. I gently pulled my arm away from her, keeping my eyes on the stranger. He was a hulking man, if I could even call him that. His eyes watched us, two brightly colored yellow and green eyes that reflected the light, giving them an eerie appearance. When he took a step forward he spoke to us with a rough, guttural voice, the tone commanding and impatient. Mary and I traded glances, not knowing what to do.

"Hello? My name is Bryn," I say, my voice soft, measured. I keep my hands visible, hoping my calm tone will reach through to them.

His words rolled off of his tongue in rapid succession. His voice was a guttural snarl, each word scraping like a blade against stone. I didn't understand the language, but the fury in it needed no translation.

He makes some kind of signal and we're surrounded by others. They drag a screaming Mary away from me and I'm forced to kneel in the tall grass. I dare a look at her, but my head is forced to look at the stranger, his hold rough and unkind. His predatory eyes study me carefully. Although he was in the shadows, I could tell he was not human. The little amount of light did nothing to hide his face's sharp angles. Dark braids framed his strong square jaw, while smooth, curved horns jutted from his forehead. I flinched when he reached out and touched my hair, caressing the strands in his fingers. A cruel smile revealed sharp canines that he snapped at me with. When he saw my fear, his chest rumbled with quiet laughter.

Mary's sobs filled the night air, a desperate, broken sound that made my throat tighten. "Please. Please, I don't want to die!" she gasped, her voice barely more than a strangled whisper

The man taunting me stilled at the sound of Mary's cries. He moved with a deliberate slowness, his face unreadable as he reached for his bow.

My stomach twisted, nausea rising like bile in my throat. "You don't have to do this! We'll leave! We'll never come back, I swear!"

Mary's ragged sobs turned to choked whimpers, her body trembling. Her lips formed half-words, breathless prayers, pleas to gods who would not answer.

I watch him nock the arrow.

I lunged before I could think, but a hand clamped down on my arm, yanking me back with brutal force. "No! Please, take me instead!" I pleaded, but he didn't even glance at me.

Time slowed. The moonlight glints off the arrow's tip, a slight tension in his jaw as he pulls back the bowstring. I could hear the sharp exhale of his breath. Mary made a small, choking noise. Her gaze found mine, wide-eyed, pleading.

Then the arrow flew.

The sound it made was a sickening, hollow *thud.* Mary let out a soft gasp, her body jolting as if the air had been knocked from her lungs. For a moment, she just stood there, swaying slightly. Then her knees buckled, collapsing into the dirt.

I didn't hear my own scream. There was only the roaring in my head, the crushing weight of helplessness, the unbearable stillness of Mary's body. I clamped a hand over my mouth, but it did nothing to muffle the ragged, shuddering sobs tearing through me. Fat tears race down my cheeks and water the ground. The leader returns to my side and grips my chin between his bruising fingers.

He looks at me and smirks. "Vekkai, Nokarr."

I tried to look around for anyone to help me, but was made to meet his eyes. I was completely and utterly alone.

"Vakkai, Nokarr," he repeated, this time in a mocking tone. A few of his companions snickered, their amusement piercing my flesh like thorns.

"Vakkai, Nokarr," I repeated. This makes him laugh, a low growling sound.

He shook his head and then pointed to himself, saying his next words with pride, "Drezhak."

Then he wipes the tears from my face, rough, almost possessive. My skin burns under his touch. His lips curl into a twisted grin. "Nokarr."

It takes me a moment to understand, but when I do, the realization hits me like a blow to the chest. He nods sharply, confirming what I already knew deep down. He's given me a name. He's not letting me go. Not ever. I am Nokarr.

CHAPTER TWO - ONE YEAR LATER
Nokarr

Smoke billowed from the rounded huts, the smell of meat cooking thick in the air. The village was arranged with the chief's home at its center, the largest of them all. He was the heart of the tribe, the balance around which everything revolved. Surrounding him were the homes of his warriors, ever watchful, ever ready to protect their leader. In this tribe, the warriors did not defend the people, they protected the chief. The rest of the Korvani scattered along the village's outskirts, their lives disposable.

This harsh reality made the Korvani rough and lethal. Every man, woman, and child had to know how to protect themselves because, in the end, no one would save them. The tribe worked in unison, performing everyday tasks like skinning the animals the hunters brought back.. Here, men and women were equal. Both shared the labor, both shared the risks. And if there was ever a disagreement, the only solution was a fight to the death. The women never won.

As I passed the members skinning fresh kills, they all paused and turned to watch me, their eyes cold and assessing. You'd think that after a year, they would have grown used to me. The crowd parts easily as I walk back home, a basket of berries resting on one hip. They spit on the ground as I pass, warding off evil spirits. The Korvani tribe was incredibly superstitious and did all they could to avoid me. They called me Nokarr, which I later learned meant "Ghost."

After Drezhak dragged me back to his settlement, I was met with hostility from the tribe. The chief, Dreshak's father, had me thrown into a pit, and left me for three days without food or water while they deliberated on what to do. I endured the taunts of the tribal women, their cruel laughter echoing as they hurled rocks at me. Bruises and cuts marked my skin, each one a reminder of their hatred. By the time they came back for me, I was half dead and Drezhak rushed me to their medicine woman. He threatened to kill her if she didn't heal me. The woman was kind enough, but she relied mostly on a young boy named Kaelen to take care of me. He was her grandson.

Kaelen was the only one who treated me like I wasn't a ghost, the only one who showed me any kindness. He was a contradiction. The tribe taught cruelty and fear, but Kaelen had a gentleness about him that none of the others shared. I sometimes wondered why he was so different. Maybe it was because he hadn't yet been broken by the Korvani ways. We became friends as I recovered. When the medicine woman released me from her care, I was taken to the chief's household and made his wife's slave. She beat me whenever I messed up, forcing me to learn the language and customs quickly. I never learned her name and it meant nothing to me. She demanded I call her 'vezar,' which meant 'master,' a title I'd never give anyone freely. But here, it was the only word that mattered. Inside, I rebelled, even if only silently.

I take the long way home, taking my time and enjoying the nice weather. The Tzaryk plains had harsh, cold winters and hot summers. The warmth on my skin was a welcomed feeling. I kept my eyes downcast because they were still sensitive to the light, though the sun here wasn't as harsh as it had been on Earth. I stroll by the river, relishing the silence and peace I rarely get at home. I'm always asked questions, yelled at or being told what to do. When I first started speaking the Korvani language, the aggressive tone and clicks made my throat raw. Now, it feels completely natural to speak. English feels foreign to me now.

"Nokarr," a hushed voice calls.

I look around and see Kaelen waving at me frantically. I jog over to him and he pulls me into the bushes. He puts his finger to his lips and points to the path I was just on. I watch Drezhak stomp past a moment later, muttering my name. He's looking for me. I hold my breath until he is gone and it's clear he's not coming back. I turn to Kaelen.

"How'd you know where I'd be?"

"You have the same ritual after picking berries. You're predictable."

I frowned, "Smartass."

He chuckles and helps me out of the bushes. We walk side by side, toward home.

"He's been looking for you all day," Kaelen says.

The vicious Korvani that killed Mary and took me prisoner. I had seen him do some horrendous things and believed he had no redeeming qualities. I knew he had taken a liking to me. While the tribe feared and hated me, Drezhak would go out of his way to get me alone. His feelings toward me weren't of innocent love, but of possession, a desire to dominate me entirely. Being his mother's slave saved me in many ways. No one was allowed to touch me, or talk to me, this included Drezhak. Kaelen had always disregarded the rule, but we were always careful. He never spoke to me around other tribe members and kept his distance. I made him promise, for his safety. He was still young, but the tribe would have no mercy and would kill him. Kaelen was like a brother to me, if something happened to him, I would never recover.

I smile at Kaelen, "I guess I'll have to change my routine."

Kaelen and I parted ways, but my thoughts remain tangled around Drezhak. Why had he been looking for me? Whatever the reason, it wouldn't be good. A knot of unease coiled in my stomach as I approached the chief's home. The moment I stepped inside, I stopped short. Drezhak was lounging on my furs, his gaze sliding lazily over me. My pulse stuttered. But then I saw her, Vezar, seated across from him, sipping her tea unbothered. Relief flooded my chest. He wouldn't dare touch me while she was here.

I flick my gaze between them, refusing to acknowledge the way Drezhak's eyes linger. I addressed her, "Vezar?"

Vezar was beautiful by the tribe's standards, her face still had sharp edges but they were softer than the male Korvani, less harsh. She has a smaller nose and delicate ears that ended in a point. Vezar kept her hair in tight locs and decorated them with the multicolored scales of the Zarjath fish. All the Korvani had tough copper skin, to blend in with their surroundings, but hers had a glimmer that always caught the sun's light.

Vezar's sharp cerulean eyes lock on me. "Drezhak has asked for your hand in marriage."

My mouth hangs open and Vezar puts her hand up before I can protest.

"I have agreed to this union."

I steal a glance at Drezhak, his eyes hungrily track

the curves of my body and I shudder. I try to plead my case.

"But, I'm yours, Vezar. Who is there to take my place?"

She gave me a harsh look, "You are nothing special."

I couldn't breathe. My ribs tightened, as if iron bands had wrapped around my chest. My mind reeled. Marriage? To him? No. No, no, no. My lips parted, but no sound came out. Drezhak's fingers dug into my hip, a possessive, brutal pressure that made my skin feel raw. I wanted to pull away, to claw him off me, but my body refused to move. Drezhak's lips brushed my neck, and I shuddered. His fangs hovered dangerously close to my skin, and I held my breath, terrified of what was to come. Just as I thought I'd lose myself to him, his mother's voice cut through the tension like a whip.

"Enough. She's not yours, yet."

An agitated growl rumbled in his chest, low and menacing, but he finally released me. Without another word, he stormed out of the hut, furious.

I shook uncontrollably, the weight of my situation finally sinking in. My mind buzzed with endless questions, but I always ended up with the same answer. Escape. It was the only way I'd survive this.

CHAPTER THREE
Nokarr

As the sun dipped low behind the snow-capped mountains, the tribe gathered for my wedding. Excitement and fear crackled in the air like a coming storm. The tribe respected Drezhak, but they could not understand why he had chosen such an *evil* woman to wed.

My heart slammed against my ribs as I stood, rigid, in my master's home. Nausea coiled in my stomach. I forced deep, steady breaths, trying to calm my nerves. I was dressed in white Kijak skin, my hair plaited into a single thick braid down my back. Vezar crushed a handful of berries, smearing their red juice across my lips and cheekbones, painting warmth onto my pale complexion.

She eyed me with cool superiority. "You are lucky to be marrying my son. He is doing you a kindness. No one else would ever want you, Nokarr."

Kindness. That was not a word I would ever associate with Drezhak. Powerful, cruel, and possessive, those were better suited to him. He was a ruthless killer, a man who respected nothing and no one. Not even me, his future wife. He had spent months belittling me, ensuring I understood how little I was worth in his eyes. And now, he would put the final nail in my coffin.

Marrying me would give him full control over my life, my body. A shudder ran through me at the thought of his hands on my skin. I *hated* him.

But by this time tomorrow, I would be far from the Tzaryk Plains.

Vezar left, satisfied with her work. Wasting no time, I grabbed my furs from the floor and began piling what little I could take– one set of clothes, a knife, some food. I wrapped them tightly in my blanket, knotting the fabric to hold everything in place.

A sudden sound at the entrance made my breath hitch. I whirled, my hands tightening into fists. But relief washed over me when I saw Kaelen standing there.

"What are you doing here?" I whispered.

"I can't let you go alone," he said.

I shook my head and walked toward the back of the hut, already moving the loose slot in the wall. "Kaelen, I don't have time for this. You have to stay here. I can't risk your life."

He stopped me with a firm hand on my shoulder. "I'm risking it. You're better than this place. You deserve to be free of it. I'll get you to the edge of Korvani lands. After that, you can disappear into the Nahtavai."

The Nahtavai. Drezhak would have a hard time tracking me there. It reminded me of Earth's rainforests, but it was deadlier. Still, it was my best chance. I exhaled, nodding my agreement. Peeking through the slot, I scanned the outside. The village was nearly deserted, all attention focused on the wedding preparations. Slipping out, I kept low, Kaelen close behind me. We scurried along the path leading to the river, our steps careful, precise.

The sound of rushing water signaled that we were close. But just as the river came into sight, Kaelen yanked me behind a massive tree, its bark scraping into my back.

His voice was barely a breath. "We follow the river to the Great Waterfall and cross where it's shallow. That's where I leave you."

"Kaelen," my throat tightened, tears threatening to spill. "Come with me."

His jaw tensed. He looked away. For just a second, hesitation flickered in his eyes, then it was gone. He shook his head. "It's better if I stay. I can cover your tracks, send them in the wrong direction."

The tears fell then. I pressed my face into his shoulder, my body wracked with quiet sobs. Kaelen was better than all of them. His kindness, his friendship- it would stay with me for the rest of my life. A reminder that I had been loved by someone on this harsh planet. That I hadn't been alone.

"Thank you," I whispered.

He pulled back and untied his necklace, pressing it into my palm.

"I can't-"

He curled my fingers around it. "Take it. Something to remember me by." His boyish smile broke through the heaviness, making me laugh through my tears.

He gripped my fist, his voice quiet but firm. "Tahvokai?"

A small, trembling smile tugged at my lips. "Tahvokai." *Family.*

Kaelen took the lead, guiding me toward the river. We moved fast, urgency pressing us forward. The sky darkened, and the farther we ran, the more I knew the truth. By now, they had discovered my absence. By now, Drezhak was coming for me.

And then, the sound I had been dreading.

A roar echoed across the plains, deep and furious. I froze, terror locking my limbs in place.

He was coming.

"Come on!" Kaelen grabbed my hand and ran with me.

My legs burned, my chest heaved with every breath, but I couldn't stop. I had to keep going. The sound of rushing water reached my ears, and I let out a cry of relief. We waded into the river, the icy current shocking my skin as it soaked through my dress. My teeth chattered. Kaelen moved further out, the water rising to his neck.

It's too deep, I realized. I'd never make it across, the current was too strong.

"I'll check for another spot," Kaelen said. He passed me and climbed onto dry land.

I tried to follow, but the weight of my soaked clothes dragged me down, slowing my progress.

Then I saw him.

Drezhak had caught up. He stood on the bank, pressing a spear to Kaelen's back.

Kaelen's expression was stoic, he would never let Drezhak see his fear. But Drezhak wasn't watching him. He was watching *me*. And he enjoyed every second of my terror.

Tears slipped down my face as Kaelen mouthed the word, '*Tahvokai.*'

A sob tore from my throat as Drezhak dug the spear into Kaelen's back, causing him to cry out in pain.

"Stop! Drezhak, stop!"

Drezhak only smiled, savoring my suffering.

"You are to be my wife. I will own you in every way. You will care for my home. Bear my children."

I nodded vigorously, desperate. "Yes! Please, just let him go. He did nothing wrong!"

Drezhak leaned in and whispered something to Kaelen. I couldn't hear it over the roar of the waterfall. Kaelen's face fell, and the haunted look in his eyes sent a tremor through me, urging me forward before the reality could settle.

Then Kaelens's voice broke through the air, sharp with desperation. "Run!"

Drezhak's spear found its mark, piercing Kaelen's heart with a sickening thrust.

"NO!"

A broken, helpless cry ripped from my throat as Kaelen gasped, his hands curling around the spear. He slowly dropped to his knees. Drezhak kicked him aside, a final, cruel twist of the knife in my heart.

Then he turned to me, "You think you can escape me, Nokarr? You will never escape. You belong to me."

I stumbled backward into the river, my body shaking. The current pulled at me, urging me deeper. Realization flickered in Drezhak's eyes.

I was going over the falls.

He lunged forward, swimming furiously to reach me in time.

I cast one last look at Kaelen, my vision blurred with tears. With shaking fingers, I tied his necklace around my neck.

Then I let the river take me.

The current yanked me over the edge, and I plunged into the Nahtavai waters below.

CHAPTER FOUR
Nokarr

The river spat me ashore, far away from Drezhak. Far away my precious Kaelen. I roll onto my back, rocks dig into my skin as I scream towards the sky, commanding it to swallow my pain. Kaelen was dead because of me. I repeatedly drove my fists into the muddy ground, fury and grief twisting inside me. I didn't try hard enough to convince him to come with me. To leave the Korvani tribe. He wasn't like them. Neither was I. I laid there forever, unable to move. I was numb from the icy river, and the complete destruction of my heart. I told myself I had to keep going. If I gave up now, Kaelen's death would have been for nothing. I slowly pick myself up, staggering into the forest. The more I walked, the more determined I became. I picked up my pace, exploring deeper into this dangerous part of the world.

My vision was clear. The dense canopy swallowed most of the sunlight, sparing my eyes from its burn. Towering trees loomed over me, vivid green and purple leaves sprouted from twisted branches that reached for miles. The sound of light rain pattered overhead, but I was safe under the protection of the trees. Lush plants lined the rough path I walked, alight like tiny fireflies, lighting my way to freedom. Hope. Something I haven't had in a long time. I pushed on, jogging now, wanting to get as far away from the Korvani as possible. I listened closely to the sounds of the rainforest. Birds called from tree to tree, warning each other of the intruder in their midst. Insects buzzed past me, one darting too close to my ear, its high-pitched whine sending me into a flailing panic. I stumbled over my own feet, catching myself just before I hit the ground.

Sometimes, I swore I heard footsteps pounding behind me. Each time, I stopped, heart hammering, scanning the trees. Nothing. Just my imagination. But it made my fear climb higher, and sent me running again. Running until I was breathless, until my legs gave out. A mist had settled over the forest floor, making my fear even more real. I wouldn't be able to hear or see Drezhak. Panic surged, clouding my thoughts, blinding me to the jungle ahead, until it was too late. A sharp sting lanced through my side. I gasped, looking down. A barb, buried in my flesh. I ripped it free with a strangled cry, but the venom had already taken hold.

It spread from the wound, burning like wildfire, seizing every muscle, turning my blood to molten iron. My body locked up. I collapsed, limbs useless, breath shallow. I watch the deceivingly beautiful flower bloom before me, tendrils as thick as vines with tiny hairlike hooks, shoot out of its center. They crawled over the ground like a swarm of snakes ready to coil their bodies around me and devour me whole. There was nothing I could do, I couldn't move. I tried, but tears only spilled from my wide, unblinking eyes. I watched in horror as they lunged, and at the last second, they were yanked back like a dog on a short leash. Straining and writhing just inches away.

I gasped in relief, my breathing had become strained. I lay on my side and watch as the world begins to tilt. Colors bled together, swirling in dizzying spirals. The jungle melted into something else, something wrong.

Distorted images made me feel like I was in a hall of mirrors. The tendrils slithered, turning into snakes. They mocked me, their hissing laughter making me shake with anger as I watched Drezhak kill Kaelen over and over again.

No. Don't show me this. I don't want to see this!

The scene goes up in smoke. Now, I stood outside my childhood home, watching my family from the window. They happily enjoy a meal together, until they notice me, then their smiles turn into Drezhaks cruel twisted smirk. He cuts them down one by one as I scream from the outside. I pound on the window, desperate to reach them, breaking the glass and slicing my hands open. The blood runs thick, pouring down, down, down into the Nahtavai river.

All of a sudden, water fills my lungs. I'm gagging, spewing water as I crawl up the bank to safety. I roll onto my back, gasping for air and gaze up at the trees. They sway drunkenly, my eyes unable to keep up with their movements.

Then everything goes completely still.

And I see it. A lone figure sitting in a tree branch above me, staring at me. Their eyes were dark as pitch, but the centers swirled with vibrant colors, reminding me of an endless, shifting galaxy. I should have been afraid. Instead, a strange calm settled over me. Who are you? I reach out and touch the scene above me, but it ripples, like a stone dropped into still water. Then I plunge into its dark depths.

Before I even opened my eyes, the sounds of the Nahtavai rushed in. My ears listened to every sound, from the soft chirps of the birds, to the breeze rustling the leaves high above me. A muffled cry, close to my ear, made me open my eyes and glance around. I scrambled away from the poor animal wrapped tightly in the flowers' tendrils. It's life, about to end in such a cruel way. It's scared, glassy eyes watch me, never wavering, as it's dragged away. I turned around, not wanting to see anymore, and when I closed my eyes all I could see were Kaelen's. *No, No, No!*

I staggered back and fell straight on my ass. I pulled my knees up and hugged them, crying endless tears. I felt like I could cry forever, in a constant state of grief. *Tahvokai.* I could still hear his voice, telling me to pick myself up and keep going. So that's what I did. I carefully navigated around the death flower and continued walking.

THE LAST FLOWER

I was on high alert, watching everything, leaving nothing to chance. I found a sharp stick that I now held in front of myself, ready to strike at the first sign of danger. My body was exhausted and my stomach gnawed at me, needing nourishment. There were berries hanging from tall, lanky pink plants along the trail. Their scent was inviting, so I tried a few, their bittersweet flavor bursting across my tongue. I ended up doubled over, vomiting behind a tree moments later.

I noticed a medicinal herb that grows near the plains, the Korvani use them to calm upset stomachs. I picked some and gingerly chewed on the roots, immediate relief washing over me. I walk until midday before coming across a hot spring and deciding to rest. I massage my aching feet, picking out twigs and thorns that embedded themselves while I ran for my life. The steaming water shimmered invitingly. I scanned my surroundings, making sure I was safe. When I was satisfied that everything was calm, I peeled off my filthy Kijak dress. I methodically drenched the skins in the water and slapped them on a nearby rock, working out the stains. Then I found sweet smelling flowers, crushed them and massaged their oils into the hide, giving it a refreshing scent. With one last dunk, I laid it out to dry where the sun shined through the trees.

For the first time, I allowed myself to relax. I slipped into the water, the heat loosens my tense muscles. I let myself feel everything. The pain and pleasure of the hot water caressing my wounds, the fear of being found by Drezhak. The suffocating memory of Kaelen's murder. A sob ripped from my throat, loud and agonized, as my tears flowed like the dam had burst. The rainforest fell silent around me, all that could be heard was my grief. I cry until my eyes are swollen.

When my tears dried, I gently wet my face, washing it all away, my sorrow mingling in the hot spring. I don't know how long I stayed in the water, floating endlessly, watching the birds in the canopy. Wishing I could fly away from here.

CHAPTER FIVE
Ezakai

This creature was getting into more trouble than a Torvahni youngling, and even they don't put themselves in danger like this. I watch the pale female. I assume it is female, judging by the softness of her curves. She was too pale for the jungle, like our twin moons, she was a bright light against Nahtavai's shadows. The female had washed ashore some time ago. When she woke, she screamed at the sky so loudly, I had to cover my sensitive ears. Her grief was obvious, unrestrained. I wonder if she had lost her husband. She wears marriage furs, though they are now coated in mud. I watch as she cries...and cries. I thought she might cry until she drowned us all, but then, without warning, the female pushed herself up and stormed into the brush.

My warriors waited for my signal. We had originally come out here for fresh water and fish, but this little creature halted our venture. Now, I wanted to know if she was a possible threat. If so, I'd end her. I click my tongue, letting my warriors know to follow. We lithely jumped from tree to tree, keeping a silent, steady pace. When we caught up to her, she was catching her breath, unaware of the deadly Pahu'rok, calculating her every move.

My warriors shift and whisper nervously as they watch the scene unfold below us. I give them a look that silences them. If the jungle takes her, then it's meant to be.

The Pahu'rok shoots a barb into her side. She gasps in pain, her eyes going wild as she rips it from her flesh. The venom works quickly, and soon, she's collapsed to the ground. She was a helpless thing. Pathetic. I watch as the tendrils reach for her, but she's too far away. Nahtavai has spared her. For now. My warriors smirk, finding her good fortune amusing. The female stares, wide eyed, oblivious to what's around her. Instead, the hallucinogen has taken effect, everything she's seeing is in her head. But it'll feel real. Her eyes darted back and forth in her head, chasing ghosts only she could see. Then, her eyes find mine, and she noticeably relaxes.

She reaches out to me, but I'm distracted when a Vorka comes bumbling through the trees, no doubt following the scent of easy prey. This is her end. She can't possibly escape her fate. She was meant to die in the jungle. I click my tongue, signaling our leave.

Then I pause. Impossible.

I watch in disbelief as the stupid animal stumbles straight into the Pahu'rok's waiting tendrils. It's quickly wrapped up, and it whines pitifully as it's brought to the ground. That should have been her.

My gaze narrows as I watch her wake with a start, noticing the dying animal beside her. After yet another pity session, she gets to her feet and continues on. I crawl through the trees watching her every move.

Don't eat those, I instinctively thought, knowing what those berries would do to her.

At least she was smart enough to only try a few. If she ate more, she would have surely died, instead of vomiting like she just did. Disgusting. And I wonder if this female is meant to walk through her life constantly toeing the line of danger. It seemed that way so far.

She finally reached the springs and scanned her surroundings, for what, I was unsure. She hesitated a moment. Then, she undressed. I looked away at first, but then I found my gaze slowly returning to the female before me. She was pale, everywhere. Her skin and hair lacked the warmth of the sun, nearly colorless except for the marks of survival. It was like she was born from stardust. Her skin gleamed when the sunlight touched it, giving it an otherworldly appearance. I forced my gaze away, irritated by the unexpected distraction. Misucca, of course, was too caught up in watching her. My friends' eyes lingered on the wrong things, things that didn't matter.

I cleared my throat and he snapped to attention. "I'm going to approach the female."

"You think this is wise?" His eyes drifted back to

her.

"If she's a problem, I'll handle it."

He nods his head, "Just call, if you need us."

I wouldn't need them. I swing down from the trees and land quietly on my feet. She doesn't notice me until I'm close enough to reach out and touch her. She shrieks, a sound that causes me to grit my teeth. The female swims quickly to the other side, away from me, and grabs a rock from the ledge. She holds the rock up, ready to use it. I smirk at her brazenness. But my amusement is short lived when she launches the rock at me and it smacks into my chest. Her face falls, and she sinks deeper into the water, trying her best to hide from me. I call out to Misucca, and a blanket falls from the trees. I retrieve it and approach her slowly. I hold it out to her, but she makes no move to come get it. I threw it to her then, having lost my patience.

"Ne'eh'ka tse?" *What do you want?*

I pause, and stare at her in shock. She was speaking the plains language. Is that where she came from? There were some differences between the plains language and mine, but we should be able to understand each other fairly well.

"Who are you?"

She pauses, clearly still distraught by my presence.

"Who are you?" I ask again, more commanding.

She swallows hard, then speaks, her voice fragile. "Nokarr."

I narrow my eyes, that can't be right. 'Ghost?'

"Where are you from?"

She avoids my eyes, "Korvani tribe."

So I was right. A plains woman. I was curious. Where was she from, really? She wasn't from this planet, that much was clear.

"Why are you not with your tribe?"

A single tear escapes, tracing the line of her cheek before she quickly wipes it away. "I was to be married to a Korvani warrior."

"You do not love him?"

She fiddles with the necklace around her neck, her fingers tracing the intricate design, as though it's both a comfort and a reminder of something she's lost. A gift from another man, perhaps? The one she truly loved, not the warrior she was to marry.

She shook her head, "No, I do not love him."

She seemed genuine. It was possible that she was running because he treated her badly. Korvani men were not known for their kindness. It's not often they take a wife, preferring fleeting pleasures, laying with any woman they want.

"Are you planning to return to the plains?"

She doesn't hesitate, "Never."

I give a sharp nod, "You will come with us. Our chief will decide what to do with you. Get dressed."

I turn to leave but stop, a thought coming to me.

I look at her one more time, and say, "I'm not calling you Ghost."

She doesn't reply, and for some time, the silence stretches between us. I think for a moment, and a name surfaces in my mind, clear, as though it had always been there.

"Seyara."

Her eyes flicker, something unreadable in them. "What does it mean?"

I don't answer her question. Instead, I walk away from her, unable to face the reason why, on this vast planet, I would choose that name for her. The memory of a flower, delicate yet strong, lingers in my thoughts. She dresses quickly, then falls into step beside me.

CHAPTER SIX
Ezakai

The female walks incredibly slow. We have to slow down just so she can keep up. I should have left her in the forest. She struggles to walk beside me, her short legs unable to keep up with my long strides. She wears her marriage furs, the scent of blood and sweat clinging to them, no matter how hard she tries to clean them. I watch her carefully, gauging her reaction to my home. It's clear she's unfamiliar with the Nahtavai. Her mystified expression as she watches the Meechins climb, using their four arms to pull themselves higher in the canopy, tells me all I need to know. Every time we come across another animal, she watches, her silent appreciation resonating with me. This is my home, and I often find myself still enchanted by it.

I glance at Seyara and give her a pointed look when I find her already looking at me.

"What, female?"

Her stunning pale purple eyes narrow at me. "I thought you said my name was Seyara."

Smart-mouthed female. "Truth."

She walks closer, making a point to stay away from my warriors. They watch her carefully, curious, but apparently, this makes her uncomfortable. I release a short, sharp cry that makes them face forward. Seyara flinches at the sound, and a small smirk pulls at my lips.

"How long have you lived with the Korvani?"

"Too long."

I'm anxious to learn more about her. She isn't cruel like the plains tribes. *How did she survive them?* I'll never find out if she keeps answering like this.

"That wasn't an answer."

"Sure it is. I was with them too long, so I left."

"Because you were getting married—"

"—forced into marriage."

So, she had no choice in the matter.

"Who were you to marry?"

She falls silent for a moment, fidgeting with the tassels on her dress before looking at me. "Drezhak. He's the chief's son of the Korvani tribe."

My warriors exchange a look. We all know who Drezhak is. He's a killer, with no care for anything living. He enjoys starting tribe wars, and there's no doubt in my mind he would start one with us if he found out we had her. I'm curious about something else.

"How did you survive him?"

"I was a slave to his parents. He wasn't allowed to touch or speak to me. It kept me safe... until it didn't."

"So you ran."

"Yes."

"And you think living a life alone in Nahtavai will be better?"

Seyara holds my gaze, a deep sadness lingering in her eyes. "Anything would be better than returning to the Korvani tribe."

Her hand goes to her necklace again, something else I'm curious about, but I decide to leave it alone. For now.

We arrive at the edge of the village, and I watch as Seyara takes in my home for the first time. Torvahni build their homes high up in the trees. The bridges creak and sway under the weight of the villagers. The wood planks and vines are still strong, centuries later. They extend from one home to the next, connecting the whole tribe in a web of walkways and paths. Giant leaves overhead protect our homes from the rainstorms and provide small washing pools when they pass.

I watch my fellow tribemates start the climb to the village, and I go to join them until Misucca nods to the helpless female.

I release a deep breath, annoyed at what I'm about to do.

"Climb on my back."

Seyara just looks at me, blinking.

"Did you not hear me?"

"I heard you. I was just wondering why you think I'd be able to climb on your back. You're so much taller than I am!"

I frown, not optimistic about her survival here. My jaw tenses as I drop to my knees so she can wrap her puny arms around my neck. The warmth of her skin against my back sends an unwanted shiver down my spine, but I shake it off and start climbing. I dig my claws in and propel us up the tree. The higher I climb, the tighter she clings to me.

She buries her face into my back, her voice muffled, "Oh my God! Why do your people live so far off the ground?"

"It's safer up here. There are a lot of predators in Nahtavai. This isn't the plains. You'll do well to learn it. And quickly."

The villagers begin to notice our presence. Her presence. She was hard to miss among the colorful life of the village. She must have realized she was being watched, because she hides her face and clings to me like I'm the only thing keeping her grounded. With one last pull, I heave us onto the platform. Seyara hesitates, her gaze darting to the forest floor far below.

I stand there, the scared female hanging off my frame. "You can get off now."

"Yeah, just a moment."

After a brief pause, she slides down my back, her tiny feet touching the platform with a sigh of relief. Yet, she stays so close that I have to gently nudge her to give me some space.

"I'm taking you to see the chief, but first, I want you to meet someone."

Seyara's mind is elsewhere, her fear keeping her close to me, but her fascination with the village urging her to explore.

"Seyara, did you hear me?"

She finally looks at me, eyes wide with wonder. "Yes, I heard you."

"Good. Let's go."

I begin walking over the bridge toward my friend's home. I want Seyara to meet her. Neyara is kind and will welcome the weak female.

"You will be staying with my dear friend, Neyara."

When the little female says nothing, I glance back, only to find she's disappeared. On the other side of the bridge, her face is struck with alarm as she peers down through the slots in the bridge. I roll my eyes and make my way back to her.

"Give me your hands."

"I can't do this."

"You don't have a choice."

When her eyes flick to mine, I see a flash of anger. I bury my amusement and keep my expression composed. I hold out my hands, and she freezes, wide-eyed.

I lower my voice, "Seyara," her eyes meet mine, "take my hands. And don't look down."

She gulps loudly, closing her eyes. Slowly, she reaches out, and I take her small hands in mine. We begin to walk across the bridge. The sway causes her to tremble, and she stumbles. I catch her easily, holding her against me.

"You can do this. Stand up straight. Keep your eyes on me."

To my surprise, she doesn't resist. She holds my gaze as we move slowly across the bridge. Seyara studies my features, her eyes covering every inch of my face, and I wonder if she finds me as strange-looking as I find her. Torvahni women are tall and strong, built to protect their younglings, while Seyara is small and fragile.

Even with those things working against her,

I find myself staring into her eyes, purple like the pistil of the flower I named her after. Its petals as white as her skin, and for a moment, I wondered if her skin would feel just as silky.

CHAPTER SEVEN
Seyara

I attempt to focus on anything but the fact that I am hundreds of feet off the ground. The warrior in front of me is my only distraction. The strange swirl of colors in his eyes stirs a memory–the lone figure watching me from the trees. A calm settles over me. Had that been real? Or just a hallucination from the venom? If it was real…it was him.

The thought lingers, and I realize that I never learned his name. "What is your name?"

His ridged brow furrows, deepening the fierce angles of his face. A crest sits proudly above it, beautiful spotted feathers blending seamlessly with his thick, intricate braids. His cheekbones are high, smooth, contrasting with his slightly hooked nose. His lips are full, wider than a human's, but still soft-looking. My gaze lingers there as I watch them move. Then I notice his scowl.

"Were you even listening?" His voice is clipped, smooth but firm, velvet over steel.

I blink. "I'm sorry, no, I wasn't."

"Why ask a question if you had no intention of

listening for the answer?"

"I got distracted." I shake my head, embarrassed. "Your name?"

His narrowed eyes, making me feel like a scolded child.

"Ezakai."

I repeat the name in my mind, rolling the unfamiliar syllables over my tongue. I liked it.

We finally step off the bridge, and he immediately drops my hands. Without a word, he turns and leads the way. Villagers move around us, going about their daily tasks—cleaning kills, preparing hides for curing. I watch as small children run freely, unburdened by the constant fear of death that had plagued my life with the Korvani.

A few women eye me warily. They are tall, built like warriors, with softer features than Ezakai. One of them approaches him, speaking in hushed tones as she strokes his arm. I wonder if she is his mate or lover, but he doesn't return her affections. His expression remains passive, unreadable.

When she doesn't get the response she wants, she turns to me, her eyes narrowing with unveiled disdain before she rejoins her small group.

I exhale slowly. It doesn't matter. I won't be here

long enough to deal with them. I'll leave. I'll survive on my own.

Even as I think it, reality settles like a stone in my stomach. There was no way back to my old life. No escape.

This planet is my home now.

As we make our way deeper into the village, I notice a large home, the biggest I've seen. Smoke billows from its roof, carrying the scent of something rich and savory. My stomach tightens and growls loudly, drawing Ezakai's attention.

He gestures toward the massive dwelling across the way. "That is the chief's home. But first, you will meet Neyara."

I stop in my tracks. "Ezakai, I don't want to meet anyone. I just want to live the rest of my life in peace."

"You are in our home. The chief will decide what happens to you."

His tone is sharp. Final. It ignites something hot in my chest. *Who does he think he is?*

My voice rises. "You have no right to keep me here! If you let me leave, you'll never have to see me again."

Ezakai moves so fast, bringing us face to face. His eyes lock onto mine, watching, calculating every emotion I fail to hide.

His voice drops to a low growl. "It goes against my better judgment to keep you here. You can't be trusted." His expression hardens. "But it's not my decision."

"You should have just… left me."

A flicker of something, sympathy, flares in his brilliant gaze. Then it's gone. Ezakai schools his features, retreating into the silent warrior once more. He turns, and walks away, leaving me standing there. A gentle-looking female approaches him. She smiles as she greets him, wrapping her arms around his broad frame. He allows it, speaking to her in low, hushed tones. She glances my way, her smile soft. Then she nods. Ezakai shifts his gaze back to me.

"Female, come."

I freeze. My teeth grind together.

"Female?" My voice sharpens. "I have a name."

Not that it was my real name, but I didn't even know who that girl was anymore. It didn't matter. I just wanted to be treated like a person. I was sick and tired of being called like a dog. I planted my feet, refusing to move. Ezakai notices my defiance immediately. He bristles, approaching me with confident strides.

"Why are you not moving?"

I lift my chin, "I'm tired of people ordering me

around. I won't be a slave again."

Something shifts in his expression. A flicker of understanding, gone as quickly as it came. He watches me in silence, then gives a slow nod.

"Seyara," he started, "won't you please meet my friend?"

There is no sarcasm, no demand. Only quiet insistence.

I exhale, feeling the weight of his gaze pressing against me. And I relent. With a nod, I follow him toward the waiting woman.

Her home is small yet inviting, its walls covered in rich purple leaves layered over a sturdy frame. Moss and wildflowers spill across its slanted roof. Most of the homes are like this, but something about hers feels different. Softer. Almost... enchanting.

"Seyara, this is my good friend, Neyara," Ezakai says, his tone softer, almost respectful. "Neyara, meet Seyara."

I take a cautious step forward, eyeing her with curiosity. She extends a hand, and I take it, her palm warm against mine. A small, understanding smile curls on her lips, as though she already knows more about me than I've let on. Like Ezakai, her skin is dark gray, but where he carries a greenish sheen, hers glows with hints of blue. Her eyes are an icy shade, reminiscent of the arctic waters on Earth. Four tight braids flow down her back, decorated with delicate flowers from the trees, making her look like she belongs to the landscape itself.

As we exchange pleasantries, I can't help but think back to Ezakai's name he picked for me. I couldn't help myself, a silly thought crossed my mind. Maybe he named me Seyara because it rhymed with Neyara.

I bite my lip to stifle a chuckle. How original.

"Welcome. Won't you come in?"

"Yes, thank you."

I go to follow her inside, but stop when I see Ezakai turn to leave.

"You're not coming?"

I feel a pang of weakness, though I quickly bury it. I don't need him, but there's a comfort I can't deny when he's around.

"I have things I need to do. I'll be back for you when the sun sets."

And then he was gone.

Neyara's home was a cool reprieve from the oppressive heat. I hadn't realized just how hot I was until stepping inside. She passed me a small cloth, and I gratefully took it, wiping the sweat from my brow, arms, and legs. It was better than nothing, and I felt much better afterward.

As I stepped further into the small space, I took in everything with eagerness. The place was immaculate. A small, stone fire pit sat comfortably in the center. Plates, cups, and bowls were stacked neatly beside it. To the left, delicious-smelling fruit hung in various stages of drying. A beautiful cyan and green brindled pelt covered the floor—an animal I didn't recognize.

A small table with a large bowl of water sat on top, and beside it, an assortment of perfectly folded clothing. Toward the back of the home was a raised bed, just a few inches off the ground. It looked incredibly comfortable, covered in soft furs. I had always slept on the floor. I didn't expect much else while I was here, but when I built my own place, I'd like a bed like that.

To the right, another bed rested beside a table filled with precious stones, shiny gems, and some type of twine. Neyara must be a gifted jewelry maker. I felt a bit awkward when I realized Neyara had been watching me with keen eyes. But her friendly smile put me at ease.

She gestured for me to sit on one of the large pillows around the firepit.

"Ezakai has told me that you are from the Korvani tribe?"

"Yes. But I'm not one of them."

Her laugh is lyrical and carries through the home, "Of course you're not. I could tell as soon as I saw you."

"Why can't Ezakai see that?"

She busies herself while she talks to me. Bringing the bowl of water, a fresh cloth and a change of clothes over to where I sit.

"It is Ezakai's duty to protect the tribe. He will always put that first."

"I see."

I could understand Ezakai's hesitation to bring me back to his village. As far as he knew, I was a stranger and couldn't be trusted. But did he have to be such an ass about it?

Neyara grabs a small basket of flowers and generously drops them into the water, a lovely fragrance fills the air. It reminded me of the flowers Kaelen would leave me sometimes, just to brighten a bad day. My heart tightens with the thought of Kaelen and I instinctively touch the necklace. Neyara notices and a look of quiet understanding reads on her face.

Her voice was gentle and kind, "Who is he?"

"He was my best friend." I pause to wipe away fresh tears. I sniffle. "His name was Kaelen. He helped me escape."

She quietly lit a wick and raised it to the heavens, "We thank Kaelen for his kindness and bravery." Then she blew it out, the smoke escaping through the flap in the roof.

I wasn't sure how much Neyara knew, or if she sensed Kaelen was gone, but the quiet respect she showed him meant more to me than I could express. He was the reason I was still alive.

"I will give you privacy to clean up and change into fresh clothes." She settled a hand on my shoulder, her touch grounding me. "Take your time. After, you may choose a bed to sleep in. You must be exhausted after everything you've been through."

She turns to leave, but I reach out, lightly touching her hand. "Thank you."

She nods kindly before slipping quietly out of her home.

I peel off the disgusting wedding furs and toss them into the fire pit. A moment later, flames rise, devouring them. I watch, mesmerized, as the last remnants of the Korvani tribe–their taunts, their cruelty, Drezhak– turn to ash. When it's over, I swear I feel something click back into place inside me. A piece of myself returned, never to be taken again.

I dunk the cloth in the fragrant water and

scrub until my skin is warm, a rosy flush rising to the surface. Then I submerge my hair, massaging the flower oils into my scalp, working through the tangles with my fingers before rinsing and squeezing out the water.

The soft, knee-length skirt and cropped top Nayara set out for me fit perfectly. The light brown hide contrasts against my pale skin, though the skirt falls to my knees instead of mid-thigh like hers–she's taller than me, after all. I plait my damp hair into a thick braid to keep it from tangling again.

Then, I sink onto the bed. The weight of the past few days crashes down on me all at once, and my body gives in. My eyelids are heavy, my limbs sinking into the soft furs.

I know I can't stay here forever. But if I could just sleep, just for a little while.

And with that last thought, I surrender to the darkness.

CHAPTER EIGHT
Seyara

Something grabs my arm. Firm. Unyielding.

I wake with a sharp inhale, the remnants of sleep tangled in my thoughts. Panic surges before reason can take hold, and I lash out on instinct. My palm connects with solid flesh, a sharp slap that echoes in the silence.

The hand releases me.

I scramble back, heart hammering against my ribs. My vision sharpens, and I find him looming over me, broad and still as stone. Ezakai. His ridged brow is drawn low, shadowing his fierce eyes. He says nothing. His expression is unreadable, neither anger nor amusement, just quiet and unsettling.

I swallow hard, pulse still racing. "You scared me." My voice is hoarse, edged with lingering fear.

"You struck me." His tone is calm, too calm.

I press my lips together, fingers curling into the furs beneath me. "You grabbed me."

"You wouldn't wake up."

I glare, my skin still prickling with the ghost of his touch. He watches me for another beat, then exhales through his nose, unimpressed. "Come. The chief is waiting."

The words land like a stone in my stomach.

I follow Ezakai through the village. The twin moons cast their silvery light over the treetops, and tiny glows of shimmering colors dot the branches, turning the village into a breathtaking display of untold beauty. The air hums with life, villagers gathered in groups, their conversations lively and warm. A sweet, smoky scent drifts through the air as young men and women pass around a pipe, laughter curling with the rising smoke. Their happiness brings a small smile to my lips.

Above us, lovers swing through the trees in a playful game of tag, their joy ending in tangled embraces. Older women sit together, watching as we pass. Their stares are unreadable, curious and knowing, like they see something I don't.

"Seyara."

Ezakai's voice pulls me back. We've arrived. I blink, realizing I've crossed the bridges without hesitation. The village at night was a perfect distraction.

He leads me inside. The chief's home is

similar to Neyara's but far larger. Instead of a bed at the back, a throne sits, crafted from twisted wood and bone, its fierce, imposing design softened by vines of blooming flowers woven into the frame. A single figure waits within, his presence commanding. Even without an introduction, I know, this is the chief.

Like the other Torvahni men, he is built powerfully, broad-chested with thick arms and legs that seem designed for both strength and agility. But where Ezakai moves with a warrior's grace, the chief carries the weight of wisdom. His graying locs frame a face lined with experience, his warm brown and golden eyes sharp with understanding. He beckons us forward.

Ezakai gestures for me to step ahead. I hesitate, then force myself to close the space between us.

The chief opens his arms, his smile creasing his strong features. "Welcome." His attention shifts to Ezakai. "Ezakai."

Ezakai bows. "Chief."

The chief's gaze settles on me. "My warrior tells me you were found alone in our home. What were you planning on doing here?"

"I escaped the Korvani," I answered. "All I want is a new life."

"Do you know how to survive in Nahtavai?"

"I survived the plains."

A low chuckle rumbles from his chest, his sharp canines flashing. "That is not the same."

I lift my chin. "Let me go, and I'll disappear."

The chief glances at Ezakai, as if weighing something unspoken between them.

"What do you think, Ezakai?"

He doesn't answer right away. His gaze lingers on me, unreadable yet searching. The scrutiny makes my skin prickle.

"She has a fighting spirit," he finally says. "But she will not survive on her own."

Son of a bitch.

"Then it's—"

"Hold on!" I cut the chief off before he could decide my fate. His frown is slightly amused, which only frustrates me further.

"Why do you even care if I live or die?" I demand.

The chief gives Ezakai a look, one I can't decipher. But he never answers me. Neither of them do.

When we step outside, frustration takes hold. I shove Ezakai, my anger boiling over. "Why did you do that?"

He doesn't even flinch. He just watches me with

that same infuriating silence.

I shove him again, harder. "Tell me! I never asked to be here! I just wanted to live my life, alone!"

Nothing.

I go to shove him a third time, but before I can, his hands catch my wrists. In an instant, I'm pressed against the chief's home, Ezakai's body caging me in.

His voice is low but powerful, a steady rumble that seems to reverberate through my bones as he stands chest to chest with me.

"You wouldn't last a day in Nahtavai."

I struggle, but he shifts his weight, holding me firm. My pulse thunders in my ears. He's too close.

His voice is quiet, but unyielding. "You will learn our ways. Then, and only then, will I let you go."

Then he was gone, melting into the night. And I was left questioning everything.

    I gave myself a moment, then made my way back to Neyara's. Sleep was elusive that night, always slipping right through my fingers. My mind wouldn't quiet, and every time I shut my eyes, his was there, staring back at me.

    When I woke, for a moment, I could almost pretend I was in a five-star hotel back on Earth. Neyara had made sure of that. The bed was soft beneath me, cradling my weight. Sunlight spilled through the flap in the roof, painting the walls with warm gold. The air was crisp, not yet heavy with heat, and the scent of flowers curled through the space like something out of a dream.

Neyara was already busy making breakfast when I joined her.

"Can I help?"

She shook her head, smiling. "No, just sit and relax. I put out some fresh clothes for you, and a pair of my shoes. If they don't fit, I can ask a friend."

"Thank you."

I lifted the skirt and top she had set aside, turning them over in my hands. They were simple but soft, and just my size.

"Ezakai dropped those off for you."

My jaw clenched. "Probably trying to make up for deciding to keep me here."

Neyara hesitated before placing a gentle hand on my shoulder. "Ezakai is right. Nahtavai is dangerous, it would be wise to stay and learn our ways."

I stared down at the clothes in my lap, frustration burning beneath my skin. I wasn't staying. The first chance I got, I would escape. If I stayed, Drezhak would find me, and then the Torvahni would suffer because of me. No. I would not let that happen. I would live on my own or die trying. And if Drezhak did find me? I would make sure I never saw the Tzaryk plains again.

Neyara guided me to the washing bowl. "Clean up before breakfast."

I dipped the rag into the cool water, letting it glide over my face and hands. The chill was refreshing against my skin, washing away the last remnants of sleep. After drying off, I reached for the clothes Neyara had set out for me. The fabric was a deep eggplant color, rich and striking. The top fit snugly, covering my chest but stopping just above my navel. I ran my fingers over the delicate tassels, admiring the craftsmanship before slipping into the matching skirt. It sat low on my hips, the fabric flowing lightly around my thighs. I tied it tightly to ensure it wouldn't slip.

"Just lovely," Neyara said warmly.

I forced a small smile, unable to believe her compliment. My whole life, I had been mocked for the way I looked. It was hard to imagine that would suddenly change.

"Thank you," I murmured.

Neyara and I sat together for breakfast. She had prepared an assortment of food– dried fruits, smoked meat, and something new. A nut she pulled from the root of a plant. She cracked it open and handed it to me. The taste was rich and buttery, like a sweetened macadamia.

"These grow everywhere on the forest floor," Neyara explained.

I tucked that bit of knowledge away. It would be useful when I left.

We ate until we were full, but my throat was dry and scratchy.

"Do you have any water?" I asked.

Neyara stood and retrieved the washing bowl, setting it in front of me. I blinked at it, confused.

"Do your people drink water?"

"We absorb it through our skin, so we don't need to drink as often. Why?"

She followed my gaze to the water bowl. Her eyes widened in realization.

"Oh! I'm sorry."

A laugh bubbled out of me, unexpected and light. It was the first time I had laughed in what felt like forever. Neyara grinned, joining in, and for a brief moment, the weight pressing down on my chest eased.

She quickly retrieved a pitcher and poured me a cup. I drank greedily, filling my cup five times before my thirst was finally quenched.

After breakfast, I slipped on the sandals.

They were a little big, but they worked. I tied them tight around my foot and ankle to keep them from budging, then followed Neyara out into the heat. We wove through the village, passing both the old and young. Laughter and chatter filled the air, their joy infectious. They had no idea what was coming. The Korvani tribe would slaughter them. I had to leave.

"You will help collect berries and fruit today," Neyara said.

I could do that. Back in the plains, foraging was one of my main responsibilities. I followed her without question, until she led me to the ledge. My body moved on its own, instinctively stepping back.

"How am I supposed to get down, exactly?"

I didn't have claws. I wasn't agile. I could barely climb a tree in the plains without Kaelen's help, and that tree was nothing compared to this monster.

"You will climb." She pointed to an opening in the platform.

Peering through, I spotted wooden rungs fastened into the trunk like a ladder, stretching all the way to the forest floor.

"The younglings use them until they can climb on their own," Neyara explained.

I frowned. "This is embarrassing."

Neyara snorted, clearly amused. "You have to start somewhere, Seyara."

I shook out my limbs, stretched my neck, and bounced on my toes. Attempting, and failing, to hype myself up.

Neyara smiled gently. "I will be right beside you."

With a deep breath, I lowered myself onto the first rung, clinging to it like my life depended on it. My stomach clenched. Swallowing my fear, I forced myself to climb down, one slow, careful step at a time. Neyara stayed beside me, her presence a welcome distraction from the dizzying height.

"What is that on your forehead?"

Panic shot through me. "What do you mean? Is it a bug?"

She laughed. "No! It's dripping down your face."

Realization dawned, and I wiped my brow.

"Let me guess, you guys don't sweat either?"

Neyara and I shook our heads at the same time.

"Of course."

By the time the ground was close, my muscles burned. Sweat drenched me, and my breath came in hard, shallow gasps. I pushed myself to move faster, desperate to reach solid ground. I took another step, but the next rung was missing. My heart slammed into my ribs as I looked down. I was still higher than I wanted to be, and the ladder had ended.

"What the hell do I do now?"

"Jump."

"What?"

Neyara hopped down easily, landing on her feet with effortless grace. "Jump."

I muttered to myself about how this was bullshit, took a breath, and—jumped. For a split second, I was weightless.

Then strong arms caught me.

"She will never learn if you keep saving her," Neyara scolded.

Ezakai.

I scrambled out of his hold, heat rising to my face. "I would have been fine."

His gaze was piercing, unreadable. "Not from where I was standing."

Not from where I was standing. I held his stare, unwilling to look away, unwilling to let him win whatever this was. But Neyara pulled me along, and I let her.

He was always right there, in the back of my mind.

I shook the thought away. I had more important things to focus on.

The trees we arrived at were thick and lush, their branches heavy with fruit. I reached for one, round and oddly black with an incandescent sheen. Neyara plucked it from my hand and sliced it open with a knife. Inside, the flesh was a brilliant pink, its scent crisp and sweet.

"Try it."

I sank my teeth into the fruit, and my breath caught. The texture was silky, softer than a ripe mango. The taste, light and delicate, reminded me of cotton candy, but without the overwhelming sweetness. Nostalgia hit me like a punch to the gut. State fairs, sticky fingers, the hum of carnival rides, my family's laughter. The first thing I always bought was cotton candy. Every time. I devoured the fruit, licking my fingers clean, trying to make the memory last.

"Come on, let me introduce you to some of the other women."

We walked up to a group, filling their baskets with berries and laughing candidly. They were all so beautiful. Each one was colored differently, from elegant emerald to midnight blue or a fiery gold. They dressed similarly to me, though their clothes matched the color of the animal they were made from. *Did Ezakai have this dyed for me?* The thought distracted me until a sharp voice cut through the laughter.

It was the woman who had clung to Ezakai when I first arrived.

"What is she doing here?"

Neyara lifted her chin. "She's here to help, Esika."

Esika was just as stunning as the other women, but her attitude was terrible. I held my ground as she approached, and she laughed at my little act of defiance. She towered over me, her frame strong. She could probably throw me into a tree if she wanted to.

She looked me up and down, venom lacing her words. "What did they call you? Nokarr?"

She was just as bad as Drezhak. Maybe he should marry her. The women behind her giggled, whispering among themselves. Heat flared beneath my skin. My teeth clenched against the sharp anger curling in my chest.

Esika smirked at my silence, tilting her head. "So, you do show some color."

Laughter rang in my ears, my pulse quickening.

I swung without thinking of the consequences.

A solid hit, right to her face.

Esika crashed to the ground. She cupped her face, her cheek already swelling. Good.

Oh my God, that hurt like hell.

I shook my hand out before crouching beside her, voice low and biting. "You might want to fix your attitude, or Ezakai is never gonna want you."

Neyara laughed, her joy at Esika's expense.

I turned on my heel and left.

Then I ran.

My heart pounded with every step, my breath quick, my limbs burning. I wasn't staying here. To hell with them. To hell with Ezakai. My name rang out behind me, distant but urgent. I didn't stop.

And then it hit me. This was my chance.

I pushed harder, branches whipping against my skin as I crashed through the forest. The sound of rushing water met my ears, and I veered toward it. The hot spring. The place where Ezakai had found me. I staggered to the edge, bending over, hands on my knees, breath coming in ragged gulps. My heartbeat thudded wildly, but with each breath, it steadied.

Slowly, I walked to the spring and slipped into the water, clothes and all.

I didn't care.

I was free.

CHAPTER NINE
Ezakai

"Ezakai!"

I hear my name, my ears twitching at the sound. I turn away from the chief and watch Neyara push through the crowd, her eyes wide as she points in some direction I don't fully understand.

"She's gone," Neyara blurts out.

My eyes narrow. She's... understanding hits me like a punch. My jaw clenches, fighting back the anger that rises.

I close my eyes and take a deep breath. When I open them again, the chief is looking at me, amusement flickering in his gaze.

"Your little flower has gone missing. What are you going to do about it?"

I catch the way he says "your little flower," and something inside me tightens. She's not mine, I remind myself. If she were, she would have listened. She wouldn't have run. I think for a moment, then meet his gaze again, my resolve hardening.

"I'm going to give her exactly what she wants."

I track her on foot, starting from the fruit trees. I don't know how long she plans to survive out here, so I packed enough for a few days. I don't expect her to last even one. A shadow of a smile tugs at my lips when I think of what she did to Esika. Neyara told me the whole story, and wouldn't stop jabbering about it. I was impressed, and if I'm honest, there's a spark of pride in me.

I followed her footprints, but even without them, I could tell which way she went just by the trees. Broken branches hang in her wake, as if some wild animal had passed through. Fierce little female. It doesn't look like she slowed down once.

The hot spring is up ahead. That's where I'll find her. I don't plan on bringing her back. Not yet. I stay in the trees, moving unseen. I want her to think she's alone. I want to see how well she survives. I perch high above the spring in the fading light, squinting through the canopy. Where is she? I climb lower, scanning the ground— nothing. Then, across from me, movement. I sink into the shadows and watch.

Seyara is building a platform in the trees. It takes her a few attempts, but she manages to wedge five logs across two thick branches. She stretches out over them for a moment, catching her breath before lashing them together with vines. She's exhausted, but she doesn't stop. She drops to the ground, gathering giant leaves to cushion her bed. Smart. She knows the trees are safer—but she learned that from my people. I wonder how she'll manage food. She can't live on berries alone.

She ties herself to the tree before lying down for the night. Resourceful.

I'm not sure if I want her to fail or succeed. I tell myself I want to see how long she'll last. But somewhere, deep down, a part of me doesn't want to see her break. I stretch out along a sturdy branch, arms and legs dangling, and watch her until sleep finally takes me.

I woke to the sound of soft humming, Seyara's voice carrying through the trees like the wind. She had found a giant Seoka fruit, hollowed it out, and used it to store fresh water. Its meat was laid out to dry. She didn't realize it yet, but she was about to make a mistake. If she ate the Seoka fruit, she'd be sick for days. The day passed without trouble. I left briefly to relieve myself, walking through the forest and taking in its quiet strength. Everything about Nahtavai grounded me, calmed my worried spirit. And yet I was worried, I realized, worried for the little female back there.

If she proved she could survive, I'd have to let her go.

Another day passed, and restlessness gnawed at me. She never ate the fruit. Instead, she used it to lure a bird, catching and killing it. The little female was proving me wrong. She was smart and strong, nothing like the fragile girl I first met here. My chest tightened at the thought of letting her go. I inhaled deeply, the scent of fresh rain and wet soil steadying my heart.

The next day, I found myself watching her once more. I could see the weight bearing down on her shoulders. She was no longer the fierce, defiant female who had fought with Esika. *What had changed?* She tended the fire first, her movements mechanical, the crackling of the flames a distant sound to her ears. She paused to wipe her eyes. Tears?

I couldn't look away as she picked up the sharpened stone, her grip tight as she worked it against the blade. The sharp scraping sound of the rock against the stone made my chest tighten, but it was nothing compared to the soft, broken sobs that escaped her lips between each strike. She didn't even try to hide her pain.

By the time she returned to her bed in the trees, I could see the weight of the world had settled in her chest, too heavy to shake. I watched as she lay back, staring at the sky through the thick canopy, the faint sounds of the forest fading as she finally gave in to sleep. I wondered what was truly driving her tears.

I remained in the shadows, still unsure whether I should continue watching her or let her be.

Then I heard it.

Heavy footfalls disrupted the jungle's quiet.

The first man emerged, copper-skinned, the color of the plains. Korvani. Two more followed. None of them were Drezhak. That gave me a moment of relief. My new priority was keeping them away from Seyara, who was napping in the trees. I gripped my knife, watching, waiting. Holding my breath as they passed directly beneath her, still unaware.

Then she moved. Just slightly. But it was enough.

One of them knocked her right out of the tree.

I swung down, landing in front of him. My blade sliced through his neck before he could react, dropping him instantly. I catch a glimpse of Seyara fighting off one of them before a fist lands, tilting the forest sideways for a heartbeat. I ducked under his next blow, scaling his back and driving my knife deep into his spine. He stiffened, then collapsed. There was one left and Seyara was struggling against him. She screamed as he grabbed at her clothes.

No.

Rage surged through me. I crossed the space

in a single breath, slamming my knee into the back of his legs. He buckled, hitting the ground hard. My arm locked around his throat, muscle straining as I held firm, cutting off his air. He clawed at me, but my grip was unyielding, his body bucking wildly in one last attempt to break free.

One last choking gasp, and he was gone.

I throw him aside and reach for Seyara. She comes to me willingly, letting me hold her. Her body shakes with sobs, and something inside me breaks a little. I let her cry until her eyes were dry. She sits on a boulder, watching me work. I fix her bed and get it back in the tree. Then, I have her climb up and lie down, covering her with the blanket I brought. Her eyes are round with fear. I go to climb down, but she grabs my arm, silently pleading with me to stay. I'm reluctant to leave her, but I have to move the bodies before a predator comes sniffing around.

"I'll be back."

I drag the bodies away from her campsite and retrieve my knife. By the time I return, she's already asleep. I lay on the branch across from her, getting comfortable as exhaustion finally takes over. The smell of damp earth and distant rain hung heavy, almost soothing. My muscles ached, each breath deeper than the last as the adrenaline faded.

"You remind me of a cat."

I open one eye and find Seyara watching me. I lifted my head, "What is a cat?"

"It's an animal from the planet I'm from."

I completely dismiss the fact that she compared me to an animal, my curiosity now taking the lead. I knew she wasn't from here. "Where are you from?"

"A planet called Earth."

Earth.

"And what are your people called?"

"We're called humans."

Interesting.

"Do you miss… Earth?"

"Sometimes, but it's a dead planet now. I was one of the last ones to leave."

I couldn't stop myself from wanting to know more. "Then what happened?"

"Our pod crashed in the plains. Only me and one other woman survived. Then Drezhak found us."

A flare of anger rises inside me when she speaks his name. He could never deserve her.

"Then what happened?"

I hear her sniffling in the darkness, the smell of fresh tears in the air.

"Then, I was held prisoner for a year. When I decided to escape, I lost someone very close to me. Someone who didn't see me as a reject or someone that needed fixing."

"Is that who's necklace you're wearing?"

Silence lingers before she answers.

"Kaelen. He was like a brother to me. Drezhak killed him for helping me."

Maybe this was the reason why she was weeping so much today. Seyara lost her home, her freedom, and the only person she connected with on this planet, all in such a short time. And I thought she was weak when I first met her. *How could I have not seen it before?* She wasn't weak. She was surviving, surviving in ways I couldn't even begin to understand. She went from one prison to another, though my people are nothing like the Korvani. I never gave her a choice.

"Seyara... I'm sorry."

After a few moments, I think she's fallen asleep, until her small voice reaches me.

"Thank you," she hesitates before speaking again, "but you don't have to stay out here with me. Your people have done enough for me."

The words came before I could stop them, "What if I want to stay?"

"It's too dangerous. If Drezhak finds me, he wouldn't hesitate to kill you or anyone from your tribe."

"Do you find me so weak?"

"What? No! I just don't want anyone to get hurt or killed because of me…I'm not worth it."

A heaviness settled on my heart. Her self-preservation was staggering. My guess was that she spent her whole life ridiculed and being around Drezhak didn't help. He never told her how beautiful she was. My heart stopped. I think she's beautiful. The thought is sharp and unexpected, as if I've crossed some invisible line, one I can't step back from.

"You're worth it to me," the words slip out before I can stop them, and I try to sound detached, but fail miserably. She was getting under my skin, and I was letting her.

CHAPTER TEN
Seyara

"You're worth it to me."

I tensed, the confusion making my world shift beneath me. I was thankful for the darkness so Ezakai couldn't see the heat that colored my cheeks. He hadn't meant it like that. My fingers curled into the blanket, gripping the fabric as if it could steady me. I traced the outline of his body, praying that my heart would control itself. A moment of silence, with more energy than a live wire, stretched between us.

Then Ezakai cleared his throat. "Why have you stopped speaking, female?"

Great, he's back. This Ezakai I could handle, cold and blunt. The other one scares me, because he makes my heart race when it's not supposed to.

I shift in my bed until we're lying parallel. It was then that I realized he could see me in the dark. Even with the smallest hint of light, his sharp eyes reflect it, giving him a predatory gaze that makes me shiver.

"What else did you want to know?"

His eyes flash when they meet mine, "Why do you

want to live alone?"

I sighed heavily, "It's better this way. I've never fit in anywhere."

"You'd fit in with my people. They will accept you."

"Yeah, tell that to Esika."

He paused for a beat, "Esika is a difficult female, but she will come around."

"Not if you keep hanging around me."

His head lifts slightly, "Why do you say that?"

I snort a laugh, "Are you blind? She wants you."

Ezakai wasn't stupid, he had to have some inkling of her affection for him. But, on the other hand, maybe being a warrior was so time consuming, he wouldn't notice something so trivial.

Ezakai laid his head back down, keeping his eyes on me, "I don't want her..."

My heart hammered in my chest, my anxiety making me weightless.

But another moment passed, and he ended up saying nothing more.

His voice rumbles low, like the thunder in the distance, "What's the other reason you want to be alone?"

"I don't want anyone else to get hurt. Kaelen was good," I can't help the tears that fall, "he wasn't like them," my voice cracks under the weight of my pain.

The wound was still fresh, his ghost stayed with me, and in some ways it was comforting. Sometimes it was haunting.

Ezakai reaches for me, but pulls back, thinking better of it. "Did you ever have a chance to mourn Kaelen properly?"

I shook my head, wiping tears from my eyes with the corner of the blanket. "It was all so sudden. Drezhak killed him, and then I went over the falls."

This time, Ezakai sits up, the sound of his claws scratching the bark sends a chill through me. "You went over the falls?"

I nod.

"You are resilient, aren't you?"

I let that sit with me. Was I resilient? Because I felt like I was slowly breaking, piece by piece.

Ezakai doesn't wait for me to answer, instead he offers me his hand.

I hesitate, but only for a second, slipping my hand into his. He pulls me to him and helps me out of the tree. Our touch lingers for longer than it should, even after our feet touch the ground.

Ezakai gently clasps my chin, "We will put Kaelen to rest."

Something tight in my chest eases, just a little.

Then he takes my hand and leads me through the twilight forest.

I stare at the waterfall. The one that carried me away from certain death. From here, it looks like a long way down, but it hadn't felt that way. One moment I was weightless. The next, plunging into the cold water. I don't remember anything after that, not until I woke up on the rivers' shore. I pull Ezakai's blanket tighter around me, the scent of him grounding me. He stokes the fire, methodical and steady. On the way here, he gathered herbs that would be burned in place of a body, carefully choosing which ones to burn for Kaelen. I was seeing a different side to Ezakai, the one that made me rethink leaving.

Ezakai finishes with the fire and brings the herbs over to me. He holds one up that looks like a clover, "This is Tashka'ri, it will help Kaelen's spirit find peace."

The next one he shows me is colored white with bell leaves, "This one is called Ihva'shii, it represents the love and affection for the deceased."

I can't hold back the tears anymore. Ezakai places the last one in my hand. Brilliant blue leaves sprout from a red stem. "This one is for you."

I looked at him and his eyes softened, "This is called Kishta'ru, meant to bring strength and healing to those left behind."

Kaelen deserves this. Honored. Loved. Remembered. He was the only light in an eternal darkness that I thought would never go away. Never let me breathe.

Ezakai leads me to the fire with his hand at the small of my back, his constant strength making it easier to put one foot in front of the other. One by one, I drop the herbs into the fire. Each one made the fire dance and colored the hot flames white.

Ezakai reads the flames, "He was pure."

"Yes, he was."

As the fire quiets, Ezakai reaches into the embers, carefully gathering the ashes onto a large teal leaf. Without saying a word, he took my hand and led me into the shallows. He held the leaf between us.

"My people give the ashes to the river. It carries the dead's spirit to the afterlife, where they will find peace."

I cry freely as we crouch in the water. Ezakai places the leaf in my hand, his fingers curling around mine. Together, we lower it into the river. The water curls around the leaf, taking the ashes and Kaelen's spirit with it.

Ezakai's words are a whisper in the wind, "Wahna'wada Nahtavai, tuma Kaelen ro'ak."

Steady river of Nahtavai, carry Kaelen home.

I break like the sun's first rays on the horizon, shattering into fractals of light that reach across the endless sky.

Then I feel him.

Ezakai.

He's hesitant and unsure, but I close the distance between us and let him embrace me. I lean into the safety of his arms, into the quiet strength that holds me together as I finally grieved for Kaelen. My sorrow flowed freely like the winding river– until there was nothing left.

Hope.

Kaelen would want me to have hope. We wanted everything for one another. And at that moment, I made a promise.

I promised to live a beautiful life, for both of us.

We walked back to camp in silence. I was lost in thought, and Ezakai stayed on alert, scanning for any signs of trouble. I had a newfound respect for him—he was not who I thought he was. Stoic and reserved, yes, but also kind and thoughtful. A side of him I was seeing more and more. And I liked it.

Ezakai caught me watching him, and I quickly looked away, heat creeping up my neck.

"What are you thinking about, Seyara? Your next escape attempt?"

I smiled. "No. I'm thinking about how grateful I am

that you followed me."

He stopped abruptly, narrowing his eyes. "You knew I was watching you the whole time?"

"Sure did."

He laughed then—deep and mirthful, the sound catching me off guard and making me laugh in return.

Ezakai crossed his arms, sharp canines flashing as he grinned. "You have outsmarted me, little female."

I strutted past him. "Somebody had to."

The spring comes into view, the rising steam promising relaxation. I tossed the blanket to Ezakai, whose shocked expression made me chuckle. I run the last few feet and cannonball into the water. When I surface, Ezakai is casually leaning on a boulder, watching me.

"Come in!"

His expression was back to being unreadable, "No."

"Don't you ever just let loose and have fun?"

"Yes," he pointed a thumb behind him, like he was hitching a ride, "I just laughed back there."

I frowned, "Was that even fun for you, or does laughing hurt?"

He ignored me, and I decided to try something. "You should have sent one of your other warriors to spy on me. I'm sure they'd want to have some fun."

Ezakai's jaw tenses at my words. "Careful, Seyara."

My smile deepens as I tease him, "What are you going to do?"

I don't have time to react. Ezakai dives in without warning, cutting through the water with ease. I barely make it two strokes before strong hands seize my waist, pulling me flush against his chest. My stomach flutters with excitement as he rests his head on my shoulder. His breath is warm against my neck, sending a shiver down my spine.

Ezakai runs a hand through my hair, the white strands slipping through his attentive fingers.

"Come back with me."

"Drezhak will–"

"Die, if he touches you or sets foot in Nahtavai."

Ezakai slowly releases me and I already miss his warmth.

I didn't want to be alone. I didn't want to just survive, I wanted to live.

"I'll go with you."

He gave a sharp nod and pulled himself out of the water. I followed, gathering what little I had. Together, we packed my things and began the trek back to the village.

CHAPTER ELEVEN
Ezakai

I had no idea what I was doing when it came to Seyara. She was frustrating. Infuriating, even. But the more time I spent with her, the more her teasing and cleverness lodged under my skin. Not as an annoyance, but as something else entirely. She walked through the jungle, lost in a world only she can see, like she was connecting with its spirit on a deeper level. Seyara gently brushed her fingers over wet leaves and every flower she touched opened to her, lingering, until it was held back by its roots. I followed in her footsteps, watching. Mesmerized. I felt like I was seeing my home for the very first time. Nahtavai was accepting her.

When we returned to the village, I left her with Neyara. I had to speak to the chief. I hastily make my way to his home and I'm let in right away.

"Ezakai."

I bow my head, "Chief."

"What brings you here?"

"I found Seyara-"

He grins, "Your little flower."

"Yes…I mean, no," A sharp breath leaves me, my chest tight, "No."

He waves me off, "Continue."

"As I was saying, I found Seyara. She was by the hot spring. While I was there, three men from the Korvani tribe attacked her."

The chief's expression changed instantly. His brow furrowed and his nostrils flared with anger, "And what did you do?"

"I killed them."

He stroked his chin, deep in thought. Then he exhaled, looking at me, "Have Misucca and the other warriors expand the perimeter around the village. I want patrols day and night. They will come, and we'll be ready."

I bow again and without another word, I turn to leave.

I'm not surprised to find Misucca smoking Ashva. He has his arm wrapped around a female and is whispering in her ear when I approach. I clear my throat loudly and he looks at me through glazed eyes.

His voice is low and drawn out, "Ezakai, where have you been?"

"I went to find Seyara and bring her back."

His brows lifted, "Did you find the little beauty?"

My fists tightened at my side. I didn't like the fact that Misucca had found her beautiful. A sharp fear cut through me. Possessiveness. I didn't like how natural it felt. I pinched the bridge of my nose and breathed.

"Misucca, I have to speak with you. Alone."

Hearing my words, Misucca sobered up a bit and kissed the female. Then he stood and followed me to a deserted platform. He leaned against a tree trunk and lit another pipe.

He inhales deeply. The smoke curls out of his mouth and nose, making him look like he could breathe fire. "What's going on?"

"We're upping security efforts."

He pushed off of the tree and came to stand in front of me, "Why, what happened?"

"Seyara was attacked by three men. They were from the Korvani tribe."

Misucca looked into the distance, "What do you need me to do?"

"Rally the warriors. Tell them we're extending the perimeter and doubling up on the night and day shifts."

He nods his head. An intense silence hung in the air. Neither of us needed to say it. War was on the horizon and it was heading straight for us.

I dragged my feet the whole way home. I lifted the cloth and walked in, dropping my weapons as I went. The aftershocks of the fight were finally catching up with me and all I wanted to do was sleep. I was about to remove my breeches, when I heard a soft voice. My ears twitched toward the sound, trying to decipher whether I was hearing things or not.

"Ezakai?"

My chest tightened immediately at the sound of her voice. I massaged my tense muscles, "Yes, Seyara?"

"Can I come in?"

I tied up my breeches and pulled aside the cloth, revealing the small female that was as bright as a moonbeam. I stepped aside and she walked past me, trailing an intoxicating scent of Vei petals. I inhaled, tasting her on my tongue. I track her every move as she studies my home. There's not much for her to look at, I thought, suddenly embarrassed at the fact. I owned a wash bowl, table and a bed.

She turns back to me, her smile bright, but it falters slightly, "Why are your eyes so dark?"

I quickly close them, hiding the proof of my desire. "It's... I'm just really tired."

"Oh, I'm sorry. It is late," she pauses a moment and I sense her come closer. I feel her body heat. She's so close.

Her voice is soft, "I just wanted to thank you, for everything. I appreciate your strength and the kindness you've shown me. Especially when I needed it the most."

My heart rate kicks up when I feel her soft lips on my cheek. I squeeze my eyes tighter, fighting against the urge to grab her and kiss her back. Everywhere.

    She steps around me, her hand lightly brushing mine. I listen for the sound of the cloth falling back in place over the door, and only then do I open my eyes. I pressed my hand over my heart. All this time I thought she was working her way under my skin. I was wrong.

Seyara already clawed her way in, and she refused to let go.

CHAPTER TWELVE
Seyara

Ezakai's dark gaze haunted my dreams all night. I remembered how his pupils were blown, the black bled outward, erasing the brilliant color of his eyes. When I kissed him, his skin was a little rough. But in a good way. And I didn't want to stop there, I wanted to press kisses along his strong jaw. I wanted to feel the ridges and angles of his body under my lips.

"Ow!"

Neyara gave me a concerned look as I sucked the blood from my thumb, the sharp tang of iron making me gag. Damn bone needle.

She threw her head back and laughed, "You need to pay attention to what you're doing Seyara!"

"I was!"

"No you weren't. You've been sitting there the whole morning with your head in the clouds."

She wasn't wrong. I couldn't stop thinking about Ezakai, no matter how hard I tried. My thoughts always found their way back to him. I massaged my temples, focusing on clearing my mind, except for the task at hand. Neyara had enlisted me in making newborn blankets for the tribe. There were ten new younglings, and it was tradition for the midwife to sew a blanket for the little ones after they're born. Neyara loved her job, and when she wasn't delivering babies, she stayed busy making jewelry.

I tied off the last stitch and lifted the blanket for Neyara to see. The pelt was beautiful. Swirls of orange, pink, and black wove through the pelt in a striking mottled pattern. I wondered what kind of creature had once worn it.

"It's perfect. Let's pack these up and deliver them."

I was thrilled to meet the younglings and walked with a little pep in my step as we worked our way from home to home. I was thankful for the distraction, needing a break from thinking about Ezakai.

In the Korvani tribe, mother's would give birth to their infants wherever they were at the time. The women allowed their infants to cry for hours before tending to them. Most of them died within their first year, either from sickness or being killed by a predator. I remembered so many nights spent crying, listening to infants wail until their voices broke, until silence swallowed them whole. I would have died before I ever had Drezhaks children. They would have grown to be just like him, because they would have no choice. It was survive or die.

The Torvahni were different. Mothers and

fathers welcomed us with open arms, genuinely happy to see us. Before meeting the infants, each family offered us a sweet tea, its delicate warmth bursting on my tongue like sun-ripened fruit. Neyara let me present the families with their younglings special gifts and every mother cried tears of joy while the father comforted her. Every couple was full of love for the brand new life that they held in their arms. Each newborn, precious and untouched by the world, was a soft pastel shade, their skin destined to darken with time. I watched ardently as Neyara held each one and said a blessing over them for a long, abundant life.

"That was beautiful, Neyara. Thank you for letting me be a part of it," I said as we crossed the bridge to the last home.

"Thank you. And you are doing an amazing job," she pauses, then stops walking. She says her next words carefully, "but you're not going to like this next stop."

I narrowed my eyes, "Why?"

She nodded toward the house behind her, "This is Esika's home."

Esika.

My jaw drops.

I leaned in, struggling to keep my voice down, "Are you telling me that Esika was pregnant when I punched her?"

My hands flew to my face, horror flooding through me. She hadn't even looked pregnant!"

A hand patted my back, "Don't be so hard on yourself. She did deserve it."

"Neyara!"

She threw her head back and laughed, causing the birds in the trees to scatter into the sky.

"Come, you can give her the blanket."

I frowned, groaning as I slowly followed Neyara the rest of the way.

At first, there was no answer. Then, a sharp pained cry, cut through the silence. We shared a worried look, before entering the home. My gaze drifted around the home and when they finally settled on Esika, I rushed over to her side. Her emerald skin had faded to a sickly gray, and she clutched her stomach, curling in on herself. Neyara stood beside me.

I gently brushed the back of my hand across her fevered brow. Her eyelids fluttered, barely opening. "Esika, what's wrong?"

Her lips parted, but no words came. She was too weak.

I whispered to Neyara, "She has a fever."

Beside her, the infant lay swaddled tightly, its tiny chest rising and falling in undisturbed sleep

Neyara spreads out an array of herbs, her movements swift but precise, then fetches a wash bowl and clean cloth. I help her roll Esika, carefully, onto her back. With practiced hands, Neyara presses gently along Esika's abdomen. I lace my fingers through Esika's, steadying her as she trembles. Her cry cuts through the air, raw and helpless. Her body coils tight, rigid with pain. Neyara nods.

Neyara nods toward the infant, "Take the baby outside. There's afterbirth left behind. If I don't remove it, she won't survive."

I move swiftly, scooping up the youngling and tucking it close against my chest. With one last glance at Esika, I say a silent prayer that Neyara could save her, then I slip outside.

I looked down at the infant as I paced, gently rocking my arms. Its tiny nose ridges weren't yet deep enough to give it a fierce look, like the adults. I tenderly caressed the silky tuft of hair on its head. It was black as night and stuck straight up like a mohawk. My adoration for the infant grew when its tiny mouth opened in a soft yawn, before settling into my arms again. A pleasant thought surfaced, curling around my heart. *Why couldn't I have this?* I wasn't with the Korvani tribe anymore. I was safe. A family of my own wasn't impossible.

The feeling lingered, until a prickle ran down my spine. I was being watched. I glance in the trees and my eyes immediately find him. Ezakai. He's lounging in the branch above me, so I step back to see him better.

"What are you doing here?"

He looked at me, but he didn't answer right away. His nostrils flared, like he just scented something tempting, and his fingers flexed at his sides. "Checking in on Esika, for a friend."

"She's sick, but Neyara is taking good care of her," I looked down at the infant, who was starting to wake, "why don't you come see the baby?" I offered.

He mulled over my words, his gaze lingering on the infant, and then me. With a quiet exhale, he jumped out of the tree and landed quietly on his feet. He didn't make a move to come closer, but he didn't have to for me to see the change in his eyes.

"Your eyes are dark again," I murmured, unable to escape their endless depths.

He remained indifferent, but his voice sounded on edge. "I've been tired lately."

Ezakai was off. He kept his distance, straining his neck to see the infant. There was something about his demeanor and how he carried himself in that moment, like if he was fighting against the urge to come closer. I ignored the anxiety gnawing at me and nodded to the baby.

"Would you like to hold the youngling?"

He looked shocked that I asked and then a little unsure. "I've never held a baby before."

I walked up to Ezakai and placed the infant in his secure arms. "See, you're a natural."

He visibly tenses, "Seyara. I'm no good at this," he tries to hand the baby back, but I rest a hand on his forearm, his skin warm under my touch. His eyes widen, flicking from me to the infant. I had never seen Ezakai so afraid.

I look into his eyes, and they soften a bit, "Ezakai, look."

His gaze drops to the baby. Wide, sunset-colored eyes take in the world with quiet wonder. The miracle of a new life between us. We share a smile, our gazes lingering for one intense moment.

I break the contact and smile at the infant, "Sweet child."

A little arm gets free of the swaddle and holds on to Ezakai's finger, attempting to draw it into its mouth. His chest rumbled with quiet laughter, and it's the sweetest sound I've heard. One that I could listen to for the rest of my life. Watching Ezakai with the baby, something warm and treacherous unfurled inside me. Affection. For him.

I brushed off the thought, quickly, before I embarrassed myself.

"Is your friend the father?"

He bounces the baby, gently, and it eventually falls back asleep.

Ezakai looks at me, "Yes. Misucca. But he's on patrol now. I actually have to leave soon to relieve him."

The words leave my mouth before I even realize what's happening. "If she was having a baby with Misucca, why did she pursue you?"

He sighed heavily, "Misucca is a bit wild. They were together some time ago, but he was never ready to settle down. She tried to make him jealous by chasing me."

"Did it work?"

"I'd say so. She became pregnant. But Misucca was scared to become a father, so he distanced himself as much as possible."

"And now? What will he do?"

He stared at me, an air of confidence in his words. "He'll do the right thing."

    I had a feeling that Ezakai would never allow his friend to shirk his duties. It only solidified what I thought about him. He was a man of honor, and by the looks of things, he would be a wonderful father.

Neyara emerges from the home, smiling brightly, "She will be fine."

I exhale slowly, relieved that Esika would make a full recovery.

Neyara's brows ticked up when she saw Ezakai holding the newborn, "Are you ready for your own little one?"

He looks at me briefly, and the emotion in his eyes is telling. He feels it too. This inexplicable pull between us that's impossible to ignore.

Then he returns his gaze to Neyara, and hands her the infant. His voice is low, but clear, "Perhaps."

Heat surges through my veins and I'm scared that he can hear the beat of my heart over the peaceful sounds of the jungle around us. I keep my gaze on the wood beneath my feet, nervous to meet his eyes. I hear him say goodbye to Neyara. What feels like an eternity passes and my breathing quickens when his legs come into view. I suddenly want to run. His hand clasps my chin tenderly, but I can't seem to move.

His deep voice is soft, but firm, "Look at me."

I slowly lift my eyes to his. Not a swirl of color can be seen, it's completely eclipsed by the darkness. I can see myself in his eyes, a burning star in a midnight sky. He gently strokes my cheek with his thumb, the light scratch of his claw sends a thrill through me. His stare is intense, even though I'm unsure where he's looking, I can feel him burning a trail across my features.

My breath caught as he leaned in, our lips inches away from touching.

His voice was thick with desire and drawn out, "Your beauty is endless."

We both moved to close the distance when a voice cut through the moment.

Ezakai quickly backed away, but his eyes remained on me, his chest rising and falling from the rush of it all.

A tall and sinewy Torvahni man walked up to Ezakai, taking his attention off me. I recognized him from before. When they first found me. This must be Misucca.

"You forgot to relieve me," he said to Ezakai.

Ezakai pinched the bridge of his nose, "I'm sorry," his eyes flicked to mine, "time escaped me."

"Well, get your ass moving."

Ezakai gave him a pointed look, "Careful."

Misucca chuckled, "You are grumpy. More so than usual."

Then he looked at me and his expression turned softer but more serious, "How is she?"

"Neyara healed her. She is going to be fine."

He exhaled slowly, visibly relieved. "And my daughter?"

I smiled at the revelation of the baby being a sweet little girl, "She's beautiful."

Misucca's smile reached his eyes. "Thank you."

Ezakai pulled him into a hug, "Congratulations," he told his friend.

When they pulled apart, Misucca entered the home. And we were alone once more.

Ezakai took slow deliberate steps toward me, closing the distance between us.

He hesitated, like he didn't want to say the next words, "I must go now."

"I understand."

He reached for me, weaving a strong hand through my hair, pulling me closer. My breath hitched when he nuzzled his face against mine, brushing his lips against my jaw, leaving a single kiss behind. I placed a hand on his chest, feeling the strong beat of his heart beneath my palm. We stand this way, suspended in time.

Then he pulled away slightly, meeting my eyes. "I'll see you again when the morning sun crests over the trees."

I was already looking forward to it, counting the hours until I could be with him.

A small smile pulled at his lips, "Goodnight Seyara."

"Goodnight Ezakai."

Then, he was gone.

I watched him disappear into the trees, my heart fully invested for whatever came next.

CHAPTER THIRTEEN
Ezakai

Seyara was the greatest temptation. If I ever gave in, it would be to her alone. And I wanted to, I realized that now. I was orderly and disciplined, but when I was with her, she stirred chaos in my soul. And I craved it.

As I watched the sunrise from the treetops, its golden rays stretching across the land, all I could think about was how much I wanted her here with me.

I exhaled sharply, pushing the thought away. There were more pressing matters. Her safety, all of our safety, was at risk. I killed another Korvani last night. The fifth in just a few days. His two companions had escaped, and there was no doubt in my mind that they had returned to Drezhak, reporting what they had found. They were getting closer. It was only a matter of time. We needed to be ready. She needed to be ready.

The sun warmed my skin, spilling golden light over the trees. It was time to see Seyara. It was time for her to learn what it meant to be Torvahni.

We are quiet. We move with the jungle, not against it.

I stalk a large Toshan, its black-as-night coat making it nearly invisible against the forest. Its killer claws dig into the soil, its steps utterly silent.

Above me, Seyara watched intently from a low branch, her skirt rising just enough to reveal the pale curve of her thigh. I forced myself to look away, focusing on the predator below us. I cannot become distracted right now.

Stay quiet.

Suddenly, the Toshan's ears flicked up. It froze, nostrils flaring as it searched the air, its fur bristling. Without hesitation, it backed away, shifting course with the same soundless grace.

Seyara kept her voice low. "What happened?"

I gave her a meaningful look. "Even the feircest predator respects the silence of the jungle. Sometimes, the quietest steps are the safest."

A moment later, a far greater predator emerged from a copse of trees. Streaked with red, the Veka's pelt was a warning—stay away. No wonder the Toshan fled. Twice its size, the Veka would have torn it apart in seconds. Lowering its snout, it sniffed the earth, then shook out its coat and moved on. The Toshan was long gone. Not worth chasing.

"I thought we were hunting."

I frowned. "We are. And that, " I pointed toward the Veka, "that's what we're hunting."

I didn't think Seyara could get any paler, but she did. Her breath hitched, eyes wide with fear.

I stood to my full height, coming face to face with her. "You will be fine."

She swallowed hard. "I've never shot a bow and arrow before."

Without thinking, I reached for a strand of her hair, absently twirling it between my claws. It was soft, lighter than my own skin, a contrast I liked. "That is why you are learning."

She took a steadying breath and nodded.

"Follow me."

We moved through the trees, tracking the Veka from above. The Torvahni hunted from the safety of the canopy, each branch a bridge beneath our feet. Below us, the beast stopped to sniff the earth, searching for its next meal.

I placed the bow in Seyara's hands. Her eyes narrowed in concentration. We waited in silence for a while, watching the Veka. When she drew the bow back, her hands trembled, but she didn't break her focus. She aimed—then released. The arrow flew, but it veered too high, embedding itself in a tree trunk. The Veka darted into the underbrush, unharmed.

Seyara groaned in frustration, dropping her shoulders in defeat. I stepped back, letting her have a moment to process her failure.

"You're close," I said. "The first time isn't always the one."

We followed closely behind, coming to a stop, as it drank from a babbling creek. I adjusted her grip and stance. Then, standing behind her, I set a hand on her waist and pulled her back against me. Sparks of arousal ignited deep inside. I forced them down, focusing.

"Draw the string back," I murmured. "Let it touch your lips."

She obeyed, her muscles taut.

"Breathe," I continued. "You want to aim behind its ear."

Seyara exhaled slowly, her eyes locked onto the Veka. The bow strained under the pull of the string, but she held steady.

I leaned closer, my lips at her ear. "Breathe in, and when you exhale, take the shot."

A moment stretched between us, tense and waiting. Then, the arrow whistled through the air. The Veka collapsed.

Seyara gasped before letting out a squeal of pure joy. She bounced with excitement. "I did it!"

Then, without warning, she threw her arms around me.

My balance shifted, too fast to stop it. I reached for a branch, fingers grazing just short.

We fell.

The impact stole the air from my lungs. A bush broke my fall, but Seyara landed hard on top of me, her elbow jabbing into my ribs.

I groaned.

"Oh no, I'm sorry!" she gasped, mortified.

Dazed, I blinked up at her. The sun framed her in gold, setting her white hair aflame.

I reached up, running my thumb over her soft bottom lip. I want to taste her.

A smirk pulled at my mouth. "Remind me to never get in a tree with you again."

Her laughter stopped my heart.

I wanted to always be the reason for that smile.

We hauled the Veka back home, dragging its weight through the jungle. Once at the village, it was hoisted onto a platform, disappearing into the trees.

Seyara stood frozen, staring after it.

"...Seyara?"

She turned on me, eyes narrowing. "This was here the whole time?"

I bit my lip to keep from smiling. She's mad. I nodded.

"Ezakai!"

"What?" I shrugged. "You have to learn to climb anyway."

She threw her arms up. "I don't have claws! How am I supposed to do that?"

Stepping closer, I took her hand in mine, running my thumb over her blunt nails. I lifted her knuckles to my lips, pressing a chaste kiss there. "You're right."

Her breath caught, but before she could respond, I unhooked two long knives from my belt and placed them in her hands. "These should help."

She stared down at them in disbelief. "You must be

joking."

I plucked the knives from her grip, returning them to my belt as I stepped even closer.

"I am." I flash her a smile. "Why would I miss a chance to carry you?"

CHAPTER FOURTEEN
Seyara

Before I can say anything, Ezakai lifts me onto his back and begins to climb. I watch breathlessly as his powerful muscles bulge and move underneath his darker skin, claws digging into the bark propelling us higher. Every movement forces me closer, my chest pressed to his back, thighs gripping his waist instinctively. It causes a delicious friction that I can't get away from. Not this far off the ground.

Ezakai pulls us onto the platform effortlessly and I quickly slide off his back, thankful that I didn't make a fool of myself.

He turns to me, gone is the playfulness. Ezakai's expression is serious. "There is something I need to tell you."

"What is it?"

He struggles with his decision to say anything, and pauses before answering. "The Chief made security tighter after you were attacked by the Korvani. But that has not stopped their hunt. I've killed five only in the past few days."

My breath catches in my throat. They're coming after me. I knew this would happen and I still decided to stay. Tears blur my vision.

"I knew this would happen, Ezakai. The village is in danger because of me."

He quickly closes the distance and holds my face in his warm hands, "No. We are in danger because Drezhak wants something he can never have. But we'll fight it. Together."

I gazed at him through my tears, his features sharp, almost alien, yet undeniably beautiful. A sudden panic gripped me, squeezing the air from my chest. Drezhak was coming, and he would slaughter anyone to get to me. Even Ezakai. I couldn't let that happen.

I pulled away from him and started walking to Neyara's to collect my things. "I have to go."

Ezakai grips my upper arm, spinning me around to face him. "You are not leaving."

I pulled out of his grip, flush with fear and anger. "I have to! Drezhak is coming. And he will never stop."

Ezakai groans in frustration. He lunges for me, grabbing my face, his hold gentle yet firm. Backing me into a tree, the bark lightly scratching my skin, he lowers his face to mine. Hovering. Hesitating. His gaze pierces my soul. "You are not leaving me."

My blood thunders through my veins at his declaration. I can't hide from his all seeing eyes.

They take me in and shape me, turning me into something new. Someone I never thought I could be. I steady my breathing.

I'm not leaving.

This thing between us, wild, fragile, and terrifyingly real. I would fight for it. I would fight for him.

I nod, finally calm. Ezakai's features soften and he slowly drops his hands and takes a small step back.

A moment passes where the only sound you could hear was the light droplets starting to fall, and the sigh of the forest as it takes in the rain's gift.

Ezakai watches me through dark lashes. "You will be training with Misucca. I've made arrangements for you to meet with him."

"Why not you?"

A small smile touches his lips. "Because he is my best hand-to-hand and weapons fighter. I am our best hunter."

I poke him lightly in the chest. "I might take that title from you."

Before I can pull away, he catches my hand, pressing it over his heart. The steady thrum beneath my palm sends a shiver through me. A smirk plays on his lips, his sharp canine glinting. "Possibly."

Then, just as easily, he lets my hand fall and gestures for me to follow. "Misucca will be a tough teacher, but I have faith you'll do just fine."

I laugh, shaking off the moment. "Let's see if you still think that after today."

He leads me to a lone home, perched at the edge of the village, set apart from the others. From here, the view is breathtaking. The entire village stretches below, woven seamlessly into the towering trees. The Torvahni move effortlessly across the narrow bridges, their steps sure and graceful. Every platform, every structure, feels like a piece of a living, breathing network. Built with care. Sustained with love. A quiet warmth blooms in my chest.

This place... it's my home.

"Seyara?"

Ezakai's voice pulls me from my thoughts. He's standing with Misucca, so I go to stand next to him.

"I was just telling Ezakai he's going to have a little fighter on his hands when I'm done with you," Misucca tells me.

I chuckle, "Thanks for the vote of confidence."

Ezakai's face doesn't crack, he stays just as serious as ever. And secretly, I love that I'm the one he smiles for. He turns to me then. "I have to walk the perimeter. Misucca will walk you back to Neyara's when you're done. I'll see you soon."

"Okay."

Then he's gone, like smoke.

I blow out a breath and look at Misucca, "Do your worst."

Misucca clapped his hands together, the sound echoing through the trees. "Excellent."

We had been at it for hours, and my body ached with every movement. Sweat clung to my skin, but the pouring rain washed it away, leaving behind the sharp chill of exhaustion. Steam rose where the heat of my body met the cold downpour. My soaked clothes stuck to me, every breath coming heavy, but I forced myself back into the stance Misucca had drilled into me.

"Bend your knees more," he instructed. "You want to be able to bounce, move quickly. Can't do that with stiff legs."

I lowered myself slightly, adjusting my weight. "Better?"

Misucca nodded. "Okay. Hit me."

I raised my hand, aiming at his face. The slap cracked through the air, sharper, cleaner this time. My palm stung, and my shoulder ached from the force of it.

"Good," he said.

Again, I struck. Then, without warning, Misucca lunged. His hand clamped around my wrist in a practiced lock, his grip unyielding. My heart lurched, my breath catching in my throat as panic tightened my muscles.

"No." His voice cut through my fear, steady and firm. "You're not trapped. Move."

I twisted, remembering the moves Misucca had taught me, but his grip was like a vise. I couldn't go anywhere.

Misucca didn't loosen his hold. Instead, he tilted his head slightly, watching me. "You can do it. Think." Misucca says.

I cleared my mind. Moving my wrist, I worked the angle. Slowly, my wrist came free from his grip.

Misucca beamed with pride, "Better. You'll get faster the more you do it. Next, I'm going to teach you about pressure points."

He held up two fingers and pointed to his eyes. "First—the eyes. Hitting them can cause temporary blindness and pain, giving you an opening to escape." Then he tapped his throat. "A strike here can cut off their voice and mess with their breathing. A quick, sharp punch will do."

He placed a hand over his chest. "A swift kick here? Knocks the wind out of them." Then, with an almost amused look, he gestured lower. "And here? That'll drop any man to his knees."

I nodded. That was the one I wanted to use on Drezhak. I'd imagined it so many times. The thought sparked a new question. "The Korvani have horns. Is there any way to hurt them?"

Misucca looked thoughtful, "Good question. When you're dealing with an attacker that has horns, you want to aim just behind them. That'll throw them off balance."

"Good to know."

The next part of the lesson was worse. Much worse.

Misucca bound my hands together with thick vines, the rough fibers biting into my damp skin. My pulse quickened. I tried to breathe, to stay calm. But the past crashed into me, flashes of Drezhak, the sharp tug of restraints pulling me down, the sting of my knees hitting the ground.

"Seyara." Misucca's steady voice cut through my panic and I hung on to every word. They reached for me, pulling me back from the edge, "Stay calm. Work the knot."

I squeezed my eyes shut, forcing air through my nose as I tried to work the knot loose. I couldn't give up. I had to prove that I belonged here, that I could hold my own. The knot was slick, the vines wet from the rain. I used the method Misucca taught me, applying it over and over until the fibers gave way.

The second my hands slipped free, I collapsed onto my back. I dragged in lungfuls of rain cooled air.

Misucca stood over me, grinning ear to pointed ear. "Good. You'll need more practice to perfect it, but you're tough for sure."

Lying there, rain washing over me, I let the victory settle in. I *would* be ready.

CHAPTER FIFTEEN
Ezakai

I drag myself onto the platform, muscles shaking with exhaustion. Rain washes over my body as I hold pressure to my side, feeling the warmth of blood seep through my fingers. I collapse onto my back gasping for air, trying to gather enough strength to move again. A Korvani had stumbled across my path as I walked the perimeter. He came at me with a knife, the bastard, and managed to get in a hit before I ended him. I shake my head in disappointment at myself. I should've seen him coming. Pulling myself to my feet, I stagger but catch my balance, my head spinning.

I walk to Neyara's and when she sees the state I'm in she has me lay down immediately. "Ezakai! What happened?"

She starts cleaning the wound and I tense, clenching my teeth against the pain. "Korvani attacked. I killed him."

Her careful hands smoothes a salve over the cut, "It's not too deep. You should heal fully soon."

I rest my head back, closing my eyes, relieved. It could have been much worse.

I'm awakened with a tender touch on my brow. I scent her. That familiar, comforting essence that is uniquely Seyara. I slowly force my eyes open, finding her immediately. Her smile, so bright, chases away the rest of the fog in my vision. The tiredness fades.

Her voice is soft, full of warmth. "I'm so happy you're okay. Neyara told me what happened."

I breathed a laugh, "I told you I wasn't the best fighter."

Her laugh was melodic, "I'm sure the other guy looks far worse."

"He did. He's dead."

A beat of silence comes and goes before Seyara leans in, brushing a soft kiss across my cheek. "I don't know what I would have done if I lost you."

I held her gaze, "You'd survive."

She shakes her head, her eyes darkening. "It wouldn't be that easy, and you know it."

I did know. Because if I lost her, there would be no recovery.

She lifts the cloth covering my wound, and freezes.

"How…?" Her fingers hover over smooth skin, unblemished. "You were bleeding earlier. How are you healed already?"

I glance down. My side is whole, not a scar in sight.

"Do humans not heal like this?"

She stares, incredulous. "No. We don't. Sometimes it takes weeks– months."

I smirk. "You really are delicate, aren't you?"

She points a finger at me, lips curving. "Hey, I've been training my ass off with Misucca. I'm not weak anymore."

I study her, taking in the fire in her eyes, the quiet determination beneath her teasing.

"No," I murmur. "You're not."

Her whole face lights up, her voice bubbling with excitement. "Now that you're awake, I can finally tell you. I'm Torvahni now!"

I blink. "The chief came to see you?"

She nods, practically beaming. "And there's going to be a feast tonight. They're cooking the Veka I killed."

I stare at her, my chest tightening in a way I can't explain. She's one of us now. She will always be in my life.

The thought settles deep in my bones, and before I can stop myself, I smile.

"I'm proud of you," I tell her. And I mean every word.

The feast is in full swing by the time I arrive. I had left Seyara earlier, returning home to bathe and prepare for tonight. I chose dark green breeches with tasseled sides, matching shoes, and left my chest bare, save for a strap to hold my knives. Scented oil lingers on my locks and skin.

My heart hammers with every passing moment, the weight of what tonight means pressing down on me. I grab Seyara's gift and step into the night.

I searched the crowd for her. The last light of the setting sun filters through the canopy, casting long shadows over the gathered tribe. The air is thick with the smoky scent of roasting meat, mingling with the earthy aroma of fresh herbs and the sweet sharpness of Ashva. Fires roar, their flickering glow washing the forest in warmth. Laughter and voices rise in celebration, vibrant and full of life. Food is shared, drink flows freely, and the steady pulse of drumming hums in the distance.

Tonight is a happy one. My tribe gathers to celebrate its newest member.

I catch sight of Misucca and make my way toward him. He spots me, his mouth falling open in mock shock.

"Look at you! You got dressed up."

I keep my expression neutral. "Seemed like the appropriate time to do so."

He slings an arm around my neck, pulling me into his side. The scent of Ashva clings to his skin. He angles his head, eyeing me with a knowing smirk. "You can't bullshit me. I see the way you look at her."

Heat creeps up my neck. I try to pull away, but he tightens his grip.

"And I've seen the way she looks at you," he continues. "You have nothing to worry about."

I exhale sharply. "Then why does it feel like this is the hardest thing I will ever do?"

Misucca's gaze sharpens, his grip firm on my shoulder. "It's not," he says. "But it will be the best thing you've ever done."

His words settle deep. No matter the nerves twisting in my gut, I know—this is what I want. With my whole heart.

"Thank you."

"Anytime." He gestures behind me, grinning. "Now go to her."

When I turn around, the world around me slows down. She is the only clear vision in a sea of blurred colors. The chatter, the movement, the laughter fade into the background. I move toward her, keeping my strides steady and confident, even though the storm inside me rages, threatening to pull me under. Her gaze drinks me in, and a knowing smile lifts the corners of her mouth. She wears a vividly colored brindle dress with matching shoes. The fabric flows around her like a second skin, the sides tied loose enough to reveal the smooth, silky curve of her waist.

Without thinking, I reach for her, my fingers threading through her soft tresses. "You look beautiful."

Her face flushes with color, and I wonder if the rest of her body would have that same reaction to me.

"Thank you," she says, her voice soft, as she shyly tucks a strand of hair behind her curved ear. "And you look very handsome."

"Thank you."

After another moment, I snap out of the trance she has me under, offering my hand. She happily takes it, and I pull her through the crowd. The rhythmic pounding of drums echoes through the village, a deep, vibrating pulse that seems to beat in time with the quickening of my heart. As we walk, the vibrations of dancing feet rumble through the ground and up my legs. Men and women in colorful regalia spin and sway, their laughter and whoops rising above the music. The sight is intoxicating, and the warmth of the celebration fills the air. I watch her out of the corner of my eye and she looks so achingly beautiful. I never wanted anything more in my entire existence.

A slow, consuming drumming begins, and couples gather around the fire, their bodies swaying sensually together, hanging off each other's lips.

Seyara looks at me, excitement shining in her eyes. "Let's go!"

She tugs on my arm, urging me forward with a breathless laugh. I chuckle, giving in, and chase her heavenly silhouette through the shifting bodies. When I catch up, I wrap an arm around her, anchoring her to me. The beat pulses thick in the air, steady and primal. Each bang on the drum pulls us deeper, stirring something raw inside me. We sway together, our bodies pressed close, the heat between us rising like a slow-burning fire. My grip tightens at her waist as we roll our hips in sync, caught in the rhythm of something eternal.

The final drumbeat fades into quiet, the last note hanging in the air, leaving behind a warmth that pulses through the silence. Something passes between us, something unspoken but undeniable. My heart hammers in my chest as she turns to look at me. Then she smiles, and the storm inside me stills just enough for me to breathe.

"Seyara..." My voice is rough as I reach into my satchel, hesitating before drawing out her gift. "I have something for you."

She steps closer, and I unwrap it, holding it out for her to see. The circlet gleams in the firelight, carved from white bone, its crest a blend of pale purple and deep green, our colors entwined. Seyara reaches for it, but I pull it just out of reach.

"Seyara, if..." I swallow hard, my throat dry. I meet her eyes, their warmth grounding me. "If you accept this from me, it means you accept me as your mate. It's what I want, more than anything. But you have to want it too."

Her breath catches. "Ezakai..." She hesitates only for a heartbeat before picking up the circlet and placing it carefully upon her crown. Then she smiles, and the weight of everything lifts.

"Yes."

The word is barely spoken before I close the distance between us, claiming her lips. Around us, the night erupts with cheers and tribal calls, but all I feel is her. Soft, fierce, and wholly mine.

I'm barely able to pull myself away from her, but I wanted to take her somewhere special. A place that she would never forget, and that would always remind her of me. Of us.

My lips move against hers in a breathless whisper, "I want to show something."

Desire flickers in her eyes. She doesn't speak, she only lets me lead her. Away from the tribe and the glow of the reaching fires, we weave through the darkened jungle, the only lights are the Lorka flowers beaming with the moon's energy. We climb higher, reaching a small waterfall surrounded by striking white flowers with purple centers. They glow in quiet night, the flowing water sparkles like a thousand stars. Seyara is entranced, floating away from me and bending down to pluck one of the flowers between her delicate fingers.

She gently touches the flower petals, "What is this flower called?"

"Seyara."

She freezes and her gaze finds mine. "What did you say?"

I nod to the flower in her hand, slowly closing the distance between us. "The flower, its name is Seyara."

Her voice was just above a whisper, "This is what you named me after?"

I wiped a single tear away, and a small smile pulled at my lips. I was completely hers. "Your perfect skin reminded me of the petals. And the purple in the center reminded me of your eyes– that captivate me with every look you throw my way. I think my soul knew you were mine before my mind did."

I hold her face and she holds my wrists like they're a lifeline, "Ezakai."

She didn't have to tell me what she wanted, my body was already in tune with her needs without ever getting a taste. I pull her to me, trapping her in my arms, unwilling to let go. She was the brightest shooting star in my skies, burning a trail from the atmosphere and into my heart. Seyara owned all of it. Every breath, every heartbeat, All of me. I would worship her for the rest of my life. I close the distance between us, taking her lips in an all consuming kiss. She tastes sweet on my tongue and I groan from the pleasure it gives me.

We're ruined as we fall into each other. Gently pulling her down, caught between me and the soft ground below, her body quivers beneath mine. I remove her clothes slowly, savoring the soft heat of her skin as each piece falls away. I drop my head and tease her breasts with my tongue. Seyara cries out when I lightly nip sensitive skin, her body levitating off the ground.

I pull away slightly, sliding off my breeches and she watches intently. Her hands reach for me, tracing the lines of my design. Her breathtaking smile ignites something deep inside, fueling the fire that consumes every part of me. I take my time, skimming my hand across her soft skin, her body shivers and dips beneath my touch. I explore all of her– licking, tasting, pleasing cries driving me to take it further. I move down her frame, nestling in between her soft thighs. Running my tongue achingly, slowly against her core, sending me to the heavens.

    I drag my tongue slowly up her body, then claim her lips with mine, the taste of her sending my senses into chaos. I inhaled, dragging her scent into myself. The light sheen of sweat on her skin, mingling with the sweet scent of wildflowers, drowns out every rational thought.

I cup the side of her face, unable to believe a woman could be more beautiful, made of stardust and dreams. "I could touch you like this forever."

Her gaze clutches at me, unraveling the last of my restraint. She doesn't need to say anything. I already belong to her.

Her body trembles, a breathless word hanging from her lush lips, "Please."

CHAPTER SIXTEEN
Seyara

The moment he pushes into me, nothing else exists. Not the open sky above us, or the spongy ground below. In a rush of heat, the world fades away. Our breath is the same. His exhale is my breath of life, and he drinks in every moan pulled from my lips. The waterfall thunders just beyond us, only rivaled by the powerful beats of our hearts, playing the same wild rhythm. The forest around us grows still, as if the world itself holds its breath, waiting for the crescendo. I pull Ezakai closer, urging him deeper, and let him completely unravel me.

A shudder racks through him, his body bowing to mine as he follows me into the storm. Breathless and undone, lost in the depths of us.

I lay in Ezakai's strong arms, underneath the moon's halos bright against the dark skies. His body is solid under my cheek, his heart a constant, steady beat. I nuzzle my face against him, breathing in the scent of new rain clinging to his skin. I push in closer, just wanting to be a part of him forever. This sweet moment burns into my memory like a brand that will never leave me. I have never loved so fiercely in my life.

I watch him stare into the heavens and I need to know, "How do you say I love you?"

I had to ask, because the Korvani didn't have a word for it.

Ezakai gives me a curious look, "What is love?"

I hesitate, the words caught in my throat. "It's... it's something that humans say to each other when they deeply care for someone. But it's more than just words," I take a slow breath, my voice softer now, "Love is what makes us choose someone above all else."

He thinks a moment before answering, "We have a saying."

Then he rolls me onto my back, his lips just inches from mine. "Nuhka'ta a'nai serae'tu."

His lips drag over my pulse, and my breath hitches, "What does that mean?" I pant, my chest rising and falling.

Ezakai slightly pulls back, holding my gaze. His eyes gleam with love, and it almost moves me to tears. His voice is soft yet certain, "My heart walks with you."

    I cling to him with all my strength, breathing in the moment, knowing I will never let this feeling go. Then he makes love to me, each powerful stroke lulling me into a peaceful existence, while the universe grows jealous of our love.

When I wake up, the jungle is silent. The only sound is the cascading waterfall. I slowly sit up and stretch, relishing the soreness in my muscles. Ezakai stirs beside me, pressing lazy kisses along my shoulder, his sharp teeth lightly nipping my skin.

He growls low as his tongue trails up my neck, sending a shiver racing through me. "I want you again."

I smile as he slowly pushes me into the soft ground, caging me beneath his body. "Don't you have to patrol?"

He lifts his head from my navel, his midnight eyes making me breathless. A flirty smile plays on his lips as he shakes his head. "They know what's happening."

He claims my mouth, tasting me, taking what he wants.

Then he stops.

His body turns rigid above me, his ears twitching in different directions. He's listening. Without looking at me, he keeps his voice low, firm. "Get dressed."

Panic rises in me as I quickly slip on my dress. I touch his arm. "What is it?"

He finally looks at me, fear flickering across his

features. "Run back to the village."

I don't understand. And I don't have time to.

The whistle of an arrow cuts through the air.

Ezakai.

He roars in pain, snapping the arrow's shaft and wrenching it from his shoulder. His knives are in his hands in an instant. Then the forest came alive. Six Korvani emerged from the shadows of the trees, their figures materializing like daunting apparitions in the growing light.

My voice shakes uncontrollably. "Ezakai—"

He steps in front of me, his body a shield. "Stay behind me," he growls.

They circle like predators. I cling to Ezakai, my pulse hammering.

Then the atmosphere snaps.

Chaos erupts.

I'm wrenched away, arms wrapping around my wrists. "Get off me!" I scream, thrashing against the unbreakable grip.

Ezakai lunges at three attackers. His blade flashes, slicing deep into one's belly, spilling blood onto the earth. The others seize their moment —one grabs him from behind, locking his arms. Ezakai slams his head backward, crushing the warrior's nose in a spray of blood.

Then I hear it—

"Ezakai!"

Another whistle and a sickening thud as the arrow buries itself into his thigh.

My frantic gaze darts around, searching.

A slow creak of branches sound above.

I look up just as a figure drops from the canopy, landing with effortless grace.

Drezhak.

His shadow stretches long in the dim morning light, his head tilting as he takes in the scene. Ezakai on his knees, bleeding, me struggling against my captors. A sadistic smirk tugs at his lips.

I twist my wrists, working them the way Misucca taught me. When I feel a sliver of give, I wrench free. I bolt toward Ezakai, who's down on one knee. I don't make it two steps before I'm yanked back, spun around. I swing blindly, my fist connecting with a face, but it doesn't matter.

A hand clamps onto the collar of my dress, shaking me until my vision blurs.

When it clears, Drezhak is there. Smiling. Cruel. Mocking.

"Vakkai, Nokarr."

Hello, Ghost.

No.

He shoves me into waiting arms, their grips bruising my skin. My stomach twists violently as Drezhak turns toward Ezakai. No, not again.

My voice splinters like stressed glass, making me sound unlike myself. "No! Drezhak, no, please!"

The pain explodes across my face before I even register his fist moving. I crumple, my mind slipping into haze.

Ezakai's voice reaches me through the fog, thick with fury. "I will kill you!"

I force my eyes open. Drezhak looms over him, whispering something in his ear. The memory of him doing the same to Kaelen before killing him floods my thoughts.

No.

Ezakai snarls, his fierce canines bared, dripping with rage—then his body jerks as the blade sinks into his stomach. Drezhak pulls back and thrusts the knife in again. Another sickening thud reverberates through my chest as the blade finds its mark once more.

I scream, the sound tearing from my throat so

raw, so broken, that the birds flee from the trees. Ezakai's face tightens in a silent scream, and I can't stand it.

A sob wrenches free as I thrash against my captors. "No! No! Ezakai!"

Drezhak pats his shoulder, mockingly gentle. "You can keep the knife."

Ezakai gasps, hands curling around the blade. Blood spills between his fingers.

Drezhak signals, and I'm dragged away. My screams are hollow, my voice cracking with anguish. "Ezakai, no—Ezakai!"

I plead with Drezhak, but I don't even know if my words are coherent through the sobs wracking my body.

Ezakai is left kneeling in the same place we made love, his blood soaking into the soil. He collapses onto his side, his breath ragged. Ezakai's gaze locks on me even as his body begins to tremble with the weight of the wounds. I'm ripped further and further away.

"No, NO!" I thrash wildly, my nails raking over skin, feet digging into the dirt as they drag me back. I can barely breathe, my throat aches from screaming, but I can't stop.

I have to get to him. I have to.

"Ezakai!"

He doesn't move.

"I love you!"

I don't know if he hears me.

I don't know if he sees me.

And I'm terrified this is the last time we will ever be together. The thought alone shatters me.

CHAPTER SEVENTEEN
Seyara

The darkness has taken over my world. The only light is from the halos in the sky. I love it and I hate it. It's a reminder of what I had, of what I lost. I fought recklessly to crawl my way back to Ezakai, uncaring what they would do to me, until the grief completely crushed me. My body gave in, shattering into nothing. I became numb as they dragged me through the forest and crossed over into the plains. A quiet sob left my lips. This place was my hell.

Drezhak taunted me the whole way, taking all the good moments with Ezakai and infecting them with his poison.

His words were a promise, "Don't worry, Nokarr. I'll take good care of you."

I look away, refusing to meet his eyes. I didn't want anything to do with him. A vicious growl reached my ears before I was roughly turned to look at him. Drezhak grabbed my hand and placed it over his hardness, "This is going to make you feel so good."

A sudden rush of anger came over me, raging against my skin to burst out, and rain hell on him. Before I even registered moving, Drezhak was on his knees, clutching himself with a strangled gasp. The men around me chuckled quietly until Drezhak threw them all a deathly stare. He slowly stood to his full height, towering over me like the highest skyscraper.

His horns press against my brow, his voice a low rasp, dripping with sick pleasure, "You're going to take all of me, everywhere. And I'm going to enjoy your screams."

That was yesterday. Drezhak threw me into the pit, and in some sick way, I was grateful. This dark hole had become my refuge. And if Ezakai was dead, let it become my grave.

I stare up at the night sky and plead with the stars to bring him back to me.

CHAPTER EIGHTEEN
Seyara

I clutch my stomach, curled on my side, the food I ate earlier churning violently. I barely manage to push onto my hands and knees before it surges up, splattering onto the dirt. My stomach clenches with each retch, the pressure bursting capillaries in my face. I can't breathe, locked in the painful grip of my own body.

I wipe my mouth with the back of my hand and collapse against the dirt wall, ignoring the rocks digging into my spine.

Days blur together. Crying, worrying, throwing up. No order. No end. I never rest, because every time I close my eyes, I see him. Ezakai. Dying. So I fight the fatigue until my body forces me under, only to wake again, screaming for him. Then I remember where I am, and the cycle starts over. And so it goes.

The stench clings to me. My hair is stiff with filth, my teeth coated in grime. The dress barely hangs on, slipping off my body. I don't know if I'd care. I don't know if I care about anything anymore.

I haven't seen Drezhak since he threw me in here.

It's the only comfort I have as I lie back down, waiting for the next wave of nausea to take me.

CHAPTER NINETEEN
Seyara

Fifteen days.

My abdomen throbs painfully and I'm not sure how much more I can take. Every muscle aches with each move I make. I've resigned myself to lying still, unable to fight it. My body wants to die. The rain finally started, I smelled it in the wind. It starts slow, then pounds the dirt, and I would be at peace if the ground softened and swallowed me whole. I wish he was here. I wanted Ezakai to rescue me, but hope was slipping away, sinking into the dirt with the rain. I couldn't accept that he was dead, not yet.

A shadow came into view.

"Come on Nokarr."

Drezhak throws down a rope, holding tightly to one side. I refuse to move.

"Grab the rope," he growls. When he sees I'm not getting up, his jaw clenches, patience snapping. "Grab the rope or I'll come down there and make your skinny ass mine."

This makes me move. It's agony getting to

my feet. I stumble toward the rope, gripping it as tightly as I can. He begins pulling me up, his muscles bulging as he lifts my dead weight. With one last heave, I'm above ground. The wind whips my face and body with a blast of frozen air. Winter is starting in the plains. Drezhak clamps his hand around my arm and drags me through the village. I ignore the stares, the insults as they spit at the ground I walk on. I don't care what they think. I only care about one person, and he's gone.

He was gone.

The thought completely stole my breath away. The realization hit me with a force I wasn't prepared for, and I froze in my tracks. He's gone. Deep down, I knew. He would have come for me if he was alive.

He would have come.

I can't stifle the sob that escapes me, my chest tightening as the grief floods in. Drezhak ignores me, not caring how my whole existence is fracturing. I grit my teeth against the new wave of nausea, fighting to hold it together, promising myself that I would escape. Even if I died trying.

Drezhak took me to his hut, except this wasn't it. It looked too familiar.

"Where are your mother and father?"

Drezhak grabbed a clean cloth, scented oil and

a blanket. Placing everything in a basket before answering me. "They're dead."

The news threw me and also frightened me. I could always rely on his parents to offer some level of protection. Now that they're gone, I'd be entirely at his mercy. Always.

"How did they die?"

"I killed them," he says, his tone was flat, like what he said was unimportant. His calm demeanor shook me to my core. This wasn't normal.

He gripped my arm again and led me outside. We walked around the back of the hut and took the path to the river. Every step reminded me of the night Kaelen helped me escape. We passed the tree we hid behind, where I told him he should come with me. I remember the flicker of doubt that shined through his gentle eyes. I squeeze my eyes tight on the memory until it fades.

We finally reach our destination and I look at Drezhak. He nods to the river. I shake my head weakly, backing away from the frozen water, but his grip is solid.. I'm too weak to fight back.

I plead with him, pulling against his grip, fresh tears stinging my eyes. "No, please. Drezhak, don't make me do this."

He grabs my chin rough enough to break my jaw, and with his other, he rips the dress from my body. "You will do this."

Then I'm pushed into the shallows.

I hiss in pain when jagged stones slice my palms, my blood blending with the dark water. The cold shock hits me immediately, my muscles lock up, making it near impossible to stand. My teeth chatter as my body is wracked with tremors. Drezhak hands me the cloth. I take it with numb fingers, and begin mechanically washing my body, scrubbing weeks of grime away. The water stings so badly, I hope the rest of my body goes numb.

When I'm done, I go to walk out, but Drezhak stops me and points back to the river. "Your hair."

I cry, the thought of going back in makes me physically sick. My stomach clenches, my mouth floods with saliva, and I turn just in time to spit up bile into the water. After catching my breath, I force myself to submerge in the deeper part of the river. The biting cold steals my breath away, but the longer I stay under, the easier it is to stay under. I let myself escape into the recesses of my mind. Ezakai. *I would give anything to have you back.* A moment passes and the pain starts to subside and tempting black shadows edge my vision. I could do it. No fights. Just my end.

Then an image appears. Piercing eyes stare back at me. A memory of Ezakai, our bodies entwined. A fight I have to finish.

I had to fight.

I break the surface, sputtering and frantically wiping the water from my eyes. I felt reborn, the river washed away my pain, my emotions. I steel my nerves and march out of the water. I approach Drezhak and take the blanket out of his hands, tightly wrapping myself in it. I quickly walk past him, back to the village, and he lets me. Probably thinking I've given up. But as I discreetly grab a few leaves of Druuna, I smile coldly, because that's not what I'm doing at all.

Drezhak gave me fresh clothes and shoes to wear. He ordered me to make dinner and tea before he got back, busy with problems in the village. Problems his new role required him to handle. I moved quickly, my hands steady despite the weariness in my bones. The meat was tough. Good. I wanted it to break his teeth. The vegetables were roasted until they had a charred bite. And the tea... I mixed the tasteless Druuna leaves with another herb, carefully measured to ensure it would knock him out cold.

I sipped my own tea, trying to keep my composure as the minutes dragged on. By the time he stomped back into the hut, my heart was already hammering in my chest. He was angry. I didn't know why and I didn't care. He removed his weapons, storing them under his furs with practiced ease, and my pulse spiked. *Damn it.*

Stabbing him in his sleep was out. He'd feel me the moment I reached for a knife.

Drezhak sat across from me, glaring, but there was a flicker of something else in his eyes, something unsettling. He didn't notice the tea immediately, but when he drank it, I had to bite back a smile. *Too easy.*

He tried unsuccessfully to bite into the tough meat. Drezhak quickly became agitated, suddenly hurling his plate across the room, his face twisted with rage. My heart leaped into my throat. I didn't have time to move, he was on me in a split second. His hand shot out and gripped my neck, squeezing with enough force to cut off my breath.

"You did that on purpose," he growled, his grip tightening.

I opened my mouth, gasping for air, but no words came out. Panic flooded my chest as I struggled to remain conscious, my vision blurring. I had to stay calm. This was my chance. But even as I fought to hold onto my thoughts, he remained completely unfazed by the tea. I made the mistake of glancing at the pot. He followed my gaze, a knowing smile curling his scarred lips.

His grip loosened and he let me drop to the floor. I sucked in gulps of air, filling my lungs until I thought they might burst.

Drezhak stood over me, dominating, reminding me that he was in control. "Druuna does not affect me."

The words froze me in place.

He knew. And I knew I would pay dearly for it.

Drezhak's gaze swept over me, taking in my body. I tried to curl up, to protect myself, but before I could, he lunged. His grip was bruising, unyielding, as I struggled beneath him. His body crushed mine, cold and immovable. I swung my fists, but he captured my wrists with ease, pinning them above my head.

Then I felt the searing pain as his sharp teeth sank into my flesh just above my breast. A scream tore from my throat, but my body fought against him in vain.

"No!"

I sob uncontrollably. My shirt was shoved up roughly, his claws slicing through my skin, and then he bit into my side.

"Drezhak! Stop!"

I screamed until my throat was raw, until my voice cracked with the strain. Every bite left its mark, a warning to anyone who might dare to challenge him. I was his.

He left me on the floor, blood spilling from my wounds, sobbing, trembling. And then, an unnatural voice, cracked and filled with fury, broke free.

"I hate you!"

Drezhak kneeled in front of me, his hand reaching out to coat his claws in my blood. He tasted it, his pupils dilating until they swallowed the whites of his eyes.

"You're mine now," he said, his voice low, dark. "And if you ever try to escape…"

He leaned in close, his breath hot against my ear, whispering cruelly, promising. "You better kill me first, because I will hunt you to every corner of this planet."

Drezhak sent me to the medicine woman, letting me walk on my own, knowing he'd hurt me too much to be a flight risk. I tried to stop thinking about him, focusing instead on Ezakai. I replayed our night together in my mind, living in that dreamscape until I reached the medicine woman's hut. Kaelen's grandmother.

I blinked away tears before entering. The older woman looked up from mixing her ointments, and the moment she recognized me, anger flared in her eyes. But just beneath it was something else, a sadness, or something like regret. I couldn't be sure.

"What do you want, Nokarr?"

The name still stung, but I shook it off. "Drezhak wants my wounds dressed."

She nodded toward a cot in the corner, and I went to lay down. With practiced hands, she retrieved a bowl of water, a cloth, and some ointment before coming to my side. I wasn't sure what to say. She lost Kaelen because of me.

The older woman focused on the bite above my breast, thoroughly cleaning it. I clenched my teeth against the sting. The bites were deep, his vicious teeth marked me, branded me like property.

The woman didn't speak, and I couldn't take the silence any longer. It was suffocating.

"I'm sorry. I'm sorry for Kaelen."

She was quiet for a moment, then sighed heavily. Her next words completely broke me.

"He adored you."

My heart stopped at her confession, and tears sprang to my eyes. My chest ached as I relived the hell of losing him all over again. I was so tired of crying, I felt like I was slowly drowning in my tears.

She applied medicine to the first bite and moved to

the one on my side. Her wise eyes studied me, as if she could see everything in a single look.

"You were his family," she said softly. A small, sad smile pulled at her lips. "He wasn't like them. He was too good," she added, tears streaming down her worn face.

I placed a hand over hers. "I wanted him to come with me. But he decided to stay. To help me. He is my savior. Kaelen died with honor."

She sat with my words for a moment, then moved to the next bite on my shoulder.

"How did he die?"

I wiped away my tears, trying to steady my voice.

"Drezhak killed him. He was helping me find a way to cross the river into Nahtavai when Drezhak appeared out of nowhere."

She didn't need to know all the details. She's already seen what Drezhak can do.

The older woman squeezed her eyes shut, as if trying to block the truth from sinking in. "Drezhak said you killed him after using him to escape. I never wanted to believe it."

She reached over, taking my hand, her grip firm yet warm. "Kaelen always spoke so highly of you. After his parents were killed, I feared he'd become someone like Drezhak. But he stayed the same...

and you made his time here better."

I sobbed, tears flowing freely as we fell into each other's arms. Her embrace was warm, maternal. A grandmother's love. I had forgotten what it felt like.

After a moment, I slowly pulled away, keeping my hands entwined with hers. "For me, he was the only light in a very dark world."

She cupped my face gently, her touch soft and reassuring. Then, she rose and walked to her herbs.

"What is your real name?"

The question caught me off guard. I hesitated, then gave her the only name that mattered to me now. "Seyara."

She returned to my side, pressing bright red leaves into my palm. "I'm Rosira."

I curled my fingers around them, their velvet texture sending a shiver down my spine. "What is this?"

"It's for Drezhak. Just steep it with his normal tea," she said, her voice clipped.

She didn't explain further—what it was for, what it would do. I was left in silence, unsure, but hopeful that it would somehow make my life easier.

I thanked her, giving her one last hug before stepping out into the frigid air. I hurried back to Drezhak's hut, but just as I was about to enter, soft moans and heavy grunts reached my ears, pinning me in place. My eyes darted around, and in the quiet, I used the moment to hide the herb Rosira gave me. I suspected Drezhak wouldn't be pleased if he found it. I buried the leaves, marking the spot with two sticks. The moans died down, and I heard only shuffling inside.

I stood up straight just as a Korvani woman sauntered out of the hut, giving me a smug look before disappearing into another.

I inhaled deeply and stepped inside. Drezhak was half-naked, just finishing pulling up his breeches, the fabric rustling as he tied them. I quickly averted my gaze, not wanting to linger on him longer than necessary. He moved toward me, gripping my shoulders, his eyes roaming over Rosira's work. I tried to shrug off his hands, but his grip tightened.

"I will have you, one way or another." he growled.

Without another word, he took my hand and forced me onto his bed. My stomach twisted at the thought of what had happened here, their combined sweat still clung to the furs. Drezhak lay behind me, pulling me tightly into his body. I tensed, nausea rising in my throat. I never wanted his touch. Only Ezakai. Always Ezakai.

Moments passed, and I heard Drezhak's soft snore. I shifted carefully, testing how far I could slip from his grip. His growl came quickly, and his arms tightened around me.

"I'm a light sleeper. You'll have to try harder than that."

I said nothing. Instead, I silently plotted Drezhak's demise, my thoughts sharp and desperate as I drifted into uneasy sleep.

CHAPTER TWENTY
Ezakai

"I can't wait to taste her on my tongue. Does she taste good?" Drezhak whispers in my ear.

Anger twists inside me, a demon ready to burst through my skin. My growl is deep and threatening, a promise of his death. A flicker of fear flashes in his eyes, then it's gone. The first blow doesn't register, my mind not grasping what he had just done. It wasn't until the second hit that I felt my skin giving way.

Every stab of Drezhak's blade sends agony searing through me. My breath is stolen as his fist connects with my body, every time he sinks the knife in deeper, driving it home. As I struggle to catch my breath, I grasp the hilt, thinking it would steady me. I want to cry out, to release the torment that wraps around my ribs like a vice. But when I open my mouth, nothing comes out. My heartbeat pounds through every part of me, fighting to keep me alive, forcing blood through my veins. I watch, entranced, as it spills over my fingers, sinking into the earth like an offering.

A bone chilling scream slices through the haze and I turn toward it.

Seyara.

I want to move, but I can't. My body works against me, staying rigid, trapped. A heavy hand lands on my shoulder, sending fresh pain through me.

Drezhak looks me in the eye, sizing me up, smirking. "You can keep the knife."

My voice is hoarse, barely above a whisper, but he hears me. "I will find you. And when I do, you will beg for death."

A grin splits his face, but his eyes tell a different story. Nothing will keep me away from Seyara. She will always be mine. And he knows it.

It's all just a waiting game now.

I watch him leave, anger and adrenaline fueling me alone. Seyara calls my name and it kills me not to answer. A surge of dizziness takes hold and makes the forest around me spin. I can't see anything, but I can hear her.

"I love you" echoes through the fog in my mind. My vision flickers, fading in and out. I see her one last time, tear-streaked, desperate. The sight of her breaks me open all over again. As they drag my light away, the shadows reach out to claim me.

CHAPTER TWENTY-ONE
Seyara

My eyes fly open as my stomach twists, threatening to spill itself. I scramble out of Drezhak's arms before he can react and race outside. Falling to my knees, I heave uncontrollably until my body is weak and my muscles ache. I wipe my mouth as I catch my breath, only then noticing Drezhak's presence behind me.

"Are you sick?" he asks, not out of concern, but because he doesn't want to catch it.

I glanced at him, my voice clipped. "I've been sick ever since you brought me here."

Drezhak only stares, saying nothing, letting the silence stretch between us.

I push myself to my feet and walk past him without waiting for a response.

His voice rings out, gruff and harsh. I pause at the doorway. "Prepare a meal. Wash the bed furs." Then he's gone.

I blow out a slow breath and step inside. My

hand cups my abdomen, rubbing gently, willing it to settle. I breathe through the nausea, and while the food cooks, I discreetly retrieve the red leaves, steeping them in the tea. I can't spend another moment here. I fix a plate and set the tea beside it for Drezhak, then sip some water and nibble on dried fruit. My anxiety only worsens the nausea.

I hope this tea kills him.

Then I'd take Rosira and bring her to Nahtavai. And anyone else that wanted to live in peace.

Moments later Drezhak returns. And he's not alone.

It's her. The woman from the other night.

I don't know what he's up to, but I know it's nothing good.

They sit across from me, and she giggles at something he murmurs in her ear. The sound is light, almost sweet, but it makes my skin crawl. I look away, disgust curling in my gut. She leans into his chest, settling between his legs.

My heart pounds when he picks up the tea.

Slowly, he brings it to his mouth, his gaze unreadable.

The air crackles uneasily, sending a chill down my spine. Something is wrong, and every instinct is screaming at me.

Then I see it.

Drezhak grabs the woman's face, pries her mouth open, and pours the tea down her throat.

A shriek rips from my lips.

He clamps a hand over her mouth and pinches her nose shut, forcing her to swallow. Then he throws her to the floor.

"You underestimate me, Nokarr."

I crawl toward her as her body convulses, her terrified eyes locked onto mine. Tears spill down her cheeks, and I clutch her hand.

A ragged, unnatural sound escapes her as blood bubbles from her lips. Red tears spill from her eyes.

"I'm so sorry."

Her body jerks, limbs twitching. Then stillness. A final, shaken breath and she's gone.

Something inside me snaps.

I lunged for Drezhak, "You bastard! I hate you!"

I slam my fists against his chest, but he only laughs. A mocking, tormenting sound that burrows under my skin and refuses to leave. My strength crumbles, and I collapse to my knees, sobs wracking my body. The floodgates burst open, my heart breaking into something beyond repair.

She didn't have to die. She was innocent.

My voice is utterly broken when I speak. "I hate you."

Drezhak crouches in front of me, his venomous gaze locking onto mine.

"You should hate yourself," he breathes. "You did this."

Tears spill anew, guilt closing in around me like a cage.

I hate him.

Because he's right.

I watch the flames dance as they swallow the woman's body. The woman I killed. I had wrapped her in Drezhak's bed furs and slowly, gently, pulled her to the river. The sun sets in the distance, and the blaze blends into the sky with fiery colors. I let the chilling wind numb me—my body, my emotions. I don't want to feel anymore.

All of Misucca's training vanishes the moment I face Drezhak. He drags pure, unrelenting hatred from me, leaving me powerless against it. Now this woman is dead because of me, and there was nothing I could have done to stop it.

When the fire dies and only ash remains, I gather it onto a large leaf. The action reminds me of when Ezakai did this for me. For Kaelen. I want this woman to have a proper funeral, knowing the Korvani have a very different way of discarding their dead. There is no closure here—not for any man, woman, or child. It's survive or die. They don't celebrate life, nor death. They only celebrate conquest.

I feel Drezhak's gaze burning into my back, but I don't care what he thinks.

Lifting my chin, I step into the river, ignoring the biting cold as it seeps into my bones. When I lower the ashes, the current takes over, washing over her, pulling her spirit with it.

"Wahna'wada, tuma na ro'ak."

Great river, carry her home.

Let her find peace where this place has none.

CHAPTER TWENTY-TWO
Ezakai

Dark memories flood my mind. Flashes of pain, muddied colors, reaching for a light just beyond my grasp. The moment my fingers brush against it, I'm wrenched back into my body. My eyes snap open, and instinct takes over. My hands find a throat, squeezing before I can even register whose it is.

A voice, strained but familiar, breaks through the haze. "Ezakai, it's me! It's me!"

Reality crashes in. My vision sharpens, and I see Misucca's face twisted in shock. I release him at once, and he staggers back, rubbing his neck. My breath comes hard and fast.

"I'm sorry," I manage, though my voice is rough, raw.

My body aches, a phantom pain where the blade had torn into me. My hands press against my torso, but the wounds are gone. Only smooth, healed skin remains. But the rage, buried beneath weeks of forced stillness, rises like wildfire. The moment I let myself feel it, it surges through me, burning away everything but a singular truth.

He took her.

Drezhak still has her.

He will die.

I snatch my weapons, fastening my knives and spear to my body with sharp, deliberate movements. My hands shake—not with weakness, but with the force of my own restraint.

Misucca watches me, gauging my state. "I tracked them through the jungle," he says, voice steady. "They took her back to the plains."

"Then that's where I'll go."

He hesitates. "Do you really want to travel at night?"

"The shadows are my friend tonight," I say. "I'll be there by dawn."

Misucca stands, twirling a knife between his fingers before gripping it tight. "I'm coming with you."

I clasp his forearm, a silent understanding passing between us. "Thank you."

We turn to leave, but a sharp intake of breath stops us. I look up to see Neyara standing in the doorway, eyes wide with disbelief.

"You were out for so long," she whispers. "I didn't think you'd ever come back to us."

The weight of her words presses against me, but I push it aside. There's no time. I step forward and pull her into a brief, firm embrace.

"Thank you," I murmured. "I know it was your clever hands that put me back together."

She huffs, but her voice wavers slightly. "Don't you forget it."

I don't. But I don't have time to say it. Because Seyara is out there. And I'm going to get her back.

We move through the night like shadows, leaping from tree to tree, our silence as deep as still water. All I can think about is getting to her. The thought drives me faster, pushes me higher, feeds the fire in my veins. Misucca keeps pace beside me, and together, we race against the night.

CHAPTER TWENTY-THREE
Seyara

After the funeral, I walked back to Drezhak's hut, and he locked me in his arms through the night. Not once did I think of escaping again. I didn't want anyone else to get hurt or killed. He had finally broken me. Instead, I thought about Ezakai—his colorful eyes that darken only for me, his strong arms that hold me tight, the way his body brought me so much pleasure. A small smile tugged at my lips as I remembered us tumbling from the trees after I killed the Veka. But just as quickly, the smile faded, replaced by tears and anger. Guilt churned in my stomach, a sickness rising inside me, forcing me to wrench myself from Drezhak's hold and rush outside.

I barely made it before my stomach emptied again. The sun crept over the horizon, golden light stretching across the land, but it did nothing to ease the cold inside me.

I heard Drezhak approach, silent at first. Then, his voice, smooth and cruel.

"You know what I think is wrong with you?"

I pushed to my feet, refusing to look at him. My

voice came out sharper than I intended. "I don't care what you think."

He chuckled under his breath. "Oh, I think you will care very much when I tell you."

Something in his tone made my skin prickle. I turned slowly, meeting his gaze, and found a smirk playing at his lips. But his eyes—they held something deeper. Something knowing.

Drezhak stepped closer, circling me, his presence tightening around me like a noose. I stiffened as he pressed his body against my back. I struggled, but his arm clamped around my chest, locking me in place. His free hand settled on my stomach, fingers trailing lower—too low. His breath was hot against my ear as he inhaled deeply, taking in my scent. I recoiled, disgust curling in my gut, but he only laughed—a sound dark and full of possession.

His lips brushed my ear. "I knew you'd been constantly sick, assuming it was stress." He cupped my lower abdomen, his touch almost tender, but I knew better. "It wasn't until your scent changed that I knew for sure."

Fear spiked through me, my veins turning to ice. "What are you talking about?" My voice was barely above a whisper.

His next words shattered me. "You're pregnant."

My breath hitched. The world tilted beneath me.

Pregnant.

That's why I had been sick. That's why my body felt different.

A tremor ran through me as the horrifying reality settled in. My child—Ezakai's child—born into *this* place. A child raised in the Korvani's brutal world. I fought down another wave of nausea, but Drezhak had already read the storm of emotions on my face. He tilted his head, almost amused, and brushed a strand of hair from my cheek.

"Don't worry, Nokarr," he murmured. "I'll raise it as my own. And then, I'll fill you with my seed and give you many more."

Rage and revulsion exploded inside me, shattering through the fear. My body moved on instinct. I drove my heel into his foot with all my strength. He let out a furious roar, his grip loosening just enough. I didn't think—I ran.

The village blurred around me as I tore through it. Faces turned, watching, but no one moved to stop me. No one *helped*. My heart slammed against my ribs, my muscles burned, but I pushed harder. I had to make it. I had to—

A force crashed into me from behind, slamming me to the ground. My lungs emptied in a choked gasp.

Drezhak flipped me onto my back, his eyes burning with violence. His hand cracked across my face. Pain erupted, a sharp sting followed by a dull ringing in my ears. My vision blurred, spots of light dancing across the sky above me.

I fought, kicking, clawing, but he was too strong. He wrenched my wrists above my head, pinning me beneath his weight. My chest heaved, panic rising like a scream in my throat.

His lips dragged along my neck. I recoiled, gagging, and he only laughed, savoring my horror.

"I will break you," he whispered. "I will breed you. And you will be mine completely."

I cry out just as a furious, pained roar rips from Drezhak's throat. He jerks upright, reaching behind him to pull a spear from his back, his own blood slicking the spearhead. Pushing off of me, he scans the area, his eyes locking onto something barreling toward us.

I force myself up on trembling arms, my breath shallow, my body aching. I follow his gaze.

It wasn't something, it was someone.

Ezakai.

CHAPTER TWENTY-FOUR
Ezakai

I hear a cry in the distance—sharp, desperate. My body moves quickly, tearing through the grasslands, Misucca close behind. Then I see him. A hulking figure crouched over something.

I push harder, my blood surging. A second cry pierces the early morning, and I recognize it instantly.

Seyara.

Rage explodes inside me. The world blurs red. I hurl my spear without hesitation, watching it sink deep into his back.

Drezhak lets out a guttural snarl, reaching behind to wrench it free. Blood drips from the spearhead as he turns toward me.

For a moment, his expression is one of disbelief—like he's seeing a ghost. Then it twists into fury.

"You," he growls, voice thick with rage. "I should've made sure you were dead."

I flick a glance toward Misucca. "Take Seyara."

Misucca moves. I don't look back.

Drezhak and I circle each other. He twirls my spear in his grip; I tighten my hold on my knives.

"I thought I killed you," he snarls.

A dark chuckle rises in my throat. "You'll have to try harder than that."

Drezhak sneers. "I broke her, you know." He tilts his head toward Seyara, his smirk widening. "Made her beg. You think she still wants you?"

My muscles coil. My grip tightens. He's trying to bait me. It's working.

"I will carve you into pieces," I say, voice low, lethal.

Drezhak grins. "I'm going to enjoy watching you try."

He lunges first, hurling the spear straight for my chest. I twist aside, but the moment I'm distracted, he's on me. His weight slams into my torso, knocking me backward. Dirt flies up around us as we hit the ground hard.

He tries to pin me, but I buck violently, sending him sprawling. The instant I'm on my feet, I close the distance. My knife slices across his arms—then another up his chest. Shallow wounds. I don't want him dead yet.

Drezhak stumbles back, touching the blood on his chest. He laughs. "Pathetic. I expected more."

I duck under his next swing and drive a fist into his chin, snapping his head back.

"Is that more?" I spit.

He wipes blood from his mouth, eyes burning with hatred. "She will always be mine."

Something inside me snaps.

I lunge, slashing my knife across his throat —not deep enough to kill, but enough to make him choke on his own breath. Drezhak staggers, clutching his neck, gasping for air as he drops to one knee. He heaves in a ragged breath, rage and desperation flashing across his face.

I crouch low, watching him struggle. "You were never strong," I say coldly. "You just knew how to break people who were."

With a snarl, he forces himself up, swinging wildly. But he's slower now, weaker. I dodge easily and step behind him. With a swift, brutal slice, I cut deep into the backs of his knees.

A ragged cry tears from his throat as his legs give out beneath him. He crashes forward, panting, his body trembling. His blood stains the earth.

I step in front of him, towering over his broken form. Now he's at my mercy, just like I was. Just like Seyara was.

"You die here," I say, my voice calm. "Alone."

His chest heaves, desperation flickering in his eyes.

I grip my knives. He will die with no honor, and no love.

I drive a blade into either side of his neck. His body jolts. His mouth opens, but no sound comes, just a choked, gurgling rasp.

I hold my gaze on his, watching the light drain from his eyes. Watching him fade into nothing.

When I finally pull my knives free, blood floods from the wounds, soaking the earth beneath him.

I breathe deep. My chest rises and falls with each heaving breath. My vision clears. The red fades.

It's done.

As I stood over Drezhak's body, I realized the Korvani had been watching the entire time, their silent presence filling the air. An older woman stepped out from the crowd and approached me.

Her gentle hand rested against my cheek, "Thank you. Drezhak and his parents before him, terrorized us."

I swallowed, my breath steadying as I met her gaze. "Do you want to come with us?" I asked. "There's a place for you. A place for all of you." I glanced back at the other Korvani, who had begun to stir, some showing hesitant interest, others still uncertain. "You don't have to stay here."

Her gaze flickered briefly to the others before returning to him. "No," she finally said, her voice quiet but resolute. "I... I need to stay. I will help them see a new path."

I nodded, understanding. "Then you have my blessing, may you lead them to a better future."

A long pause stretched between us. She offered a small, quiet smile, and then returned to her people. As she did, I felt a sense of finality settle over me.

A gentle touch grabbed my attention, and I already know it's her. Seyara. My beautiful mate. I pull her into my arms, capturing her lips in a kiss—fierce, desperate. I need her. My hands tangle in her hair, my breath mingling with hers. She is everything. Like the moon, she pulls me into her orbit, the brightest star in my sky.

"Seyara," I breathe against her lips, pressing my forehead to hers. I couldn't get enough of her.

Her tears fall, and I catch them with my thumb, holding her face between my hands. She smiles— radiant, free. The nightmare is over.

I lift her chin, my voice low, almost afraid to ask. "Did he...?"

Her eyes soften. "No. Not at all."

Relief crashes over me. My chest tightens, and I exhale a breath I didn't realize I was holding. I pull her closer, my arms tightening around her, vowing to never let her go.

Then I inhale deeply, taking in her scent—and something different. Something new.

I freeze. My heart stammers in my chest.

She is pregnant. With my child.

A slow, disbelieving smile spreads across my face. "You're carrying my baby."

Seyara laughs, her joy like the first light after a storm. She nods. "Yes."

A sound escapes me—half a laugh, half a breath of pure wonder. I lift her effortlessly, spinning her in my arms, cherishing every heartbeat, every breath, every piece of her.

She is mine. She is safe. And now—we are more.

EPILOGUE
Seyara

"Push Seyara, push."

Another contraction urges me to push. I bear down, allowing my body to do what it needs to bring my child into this world. A guttural cry rips from my throat as pain splits through me. Sweat drips down my brow, and Ezakai is right there, dabbing it away with gentle hands. My fingers dig into his, gripping with all the strength I have left. My body shakes with the effort, my vision blurring at the edges—and then, finally, the pressure releases. A weight lifts from my body, and I collapse onto the bed, utterly exhausted.

Ezakai presses kisses to my damp forehead, his voice thick with emotion. "You're amazing."

Then we hear it—the first cries of our child, strong and piercing. Relief crashes over me, stealing the breath from my lungs. Tears burn in my eyes. Ezakai helps me sit up, stacking pillows behind my back as I reach for our baby.

Neyara wraps our newborn in a soft, fur-lined blanket and smiles warmly. "It is a boy," she announces, carefully setting him in my waiting arms.

He is so small, so perfect. His skin is a soft, light green with an otherworldly sheen, a perfect blend of Ezakai and me. I let out a shaky breath, unable to look away from him. Ezakai's large hand cradles the back of our son's head, his expression one of pure, unguarded awe. Pride and love shine in his eyes as we watch our son yawn, his tiny lips parting. And then, slowly, his eyes blink open.

My breath catches.

Purple irises blend seamlessly into a dark green edge, reminding me of the Veylora flowers that cover our home.

"He's beautiful," I whisper, running a gentle finger over his soft nose ridges and into his silky dark hair. "What should we name him?"

Ezakai lays beside me, pulling me into his warm embrace. I breathe in his scent, letting the comfort of him wrap around me.

"I was thinking... we can name him Kaelen."

I twist to look at him, tears already spilling over. "I love that."

Ezakai drops a kiss onto my lips, then caresses his son's chubby cheek. "Kaelen, the fierce warrior."

Right on cue, Kaelen lets out a loud whimpering cry and starts rooting for my breast.

I laugh softly, guiding him to me. "Right now, I think he's just Kaelen the hungry."

Ezakai chuckles, pure joy filling his voice. "Okay, maybe not a warrior yet."

My mate gently squeezes out from behind me, and already I miss his warmth. "Where are you going?"

He flashes me a charming smile. "I have something for you," then disappears outside.

I return my attention to Kaelen, watching in quiet wonder as he drifts off to sleep.

Neyara approaches my bedside, voice soft. "Would you like me to place him in his suhna?"

I nod, my heart full. Neyara carefully lifts Kaelen and places him in the little woven basket lined with furs and blankets. I was so thankful for her. She had been with me every step of the way. It took time to prepare for this pregnancy—we had no idea what to expect. By six months, I had reached full term, my body changing so fast it had stunned the tribe. But they had embraced me, supported me, further threading me into the intricate beauty of this community. Esika even made our baby a blanket, soft and vibrant, her way of thanking me for my help when she was sick. It was a gesture I hadn't expected, but it made my heart swell.

"Thank you, Neyara."

She nods, then quietly takes her leave.

I'm already drifting into sleep when Ezakai returns. He slides back into bed beside me, wrapping me in his arms again. Then, with a tenderness that makes my heart ache, he places something in front of me.

A flower.

Not just any flower. A Seyara.

The very same flower he named me after.

My breath catches as memories flood me. The first time he had given me this name, the moment I had understood its meaning. My heart swells, my fingers trembling as I take the delicate bloom between them.

Ezakai's breath is warm against my ear. I instinctively lean into him, savoring the shiver it sends through me.

"Every Torvahni male gives his mate a Seyara flower after she births their first child."

His lips brush my neck, his voice barely above a whisper. "This flower means new life."

I close my eyes, smiling as I twirl the petals between my fingers. He had given me a new life. I lift my gaze to Ezakai, and he's already there, waiting, his lips a breath away from mine.

I crashed on this planet, believing I had lost

everything. I had given up hope of ever having something more, something good. But I had found passion, love, and friendship. I had him and now our son.

My heart would walk with him for eternity.

I whisper against his lips, "Nuhka'ta a'nai serae'tu."

Ezakai smiles, brushing his thumb over my cheek. "I love you, too."

THANK YOU READERS!

Thank you for joining me on this incredible journey to Nahtavai. Writing *The Last Flower*, my very first sci-fi romance, has been an unforgettable experience, and I'm so grateful for your support along the way. Exploring Seyara and Ezakai's story, their struggles, their love, and the world they built together has been nothing short of magical. I've fallen in love with them, and I hope you have too. Your love for this story means everything—thank you for being part of it.

Follow me on Amazon and don't forget to leave a review!

You can also check out my Goodreads page here- Narcissus Blue (Author of Sedna's Anchor) | Goodreads

If you want to take a dive inside my mind and see what inspired this story and others, follow me on Pinterest- Pinterest

BOOKS BY THIS AUTHOR

Chasing Souls

Lost Soul
I've wandered unseen for so long, trapped between life and death, that I'd almost forgotten what it meant to be whole- until him. A soul-eater with a deal too tempting to refuse. In exchange for killing the witch who owns him, I get my body back. Simple. But nothing ever is. Even in flesh, I can't walk away. He's still bound, his soul lost to the underworld, and against all reason, I choose to help him. Because somehow, in all this madness, I think I've found what I was missing.

Soul Eater
I've never feared the dark. I've been a part of it for as long as I can remember. Killing to survive, bound to a master who steals what little I have left. But then she comes, a wildfire in the night, a lost soul who makes me yearn for something more. When she gets her body back, she should run.

Leave me to my fate. But she doesn't. She stays. And now we stand at the gates of Yomi, where gods and monsters wait, where the price of my soul may be more than either of us can pay.

The underworld doesn't let go easily. How far will we go for each other? And when faced with the impossible- will we survive it?

BOOKS BY THIS AUTHOR

Sedna's Anchor

Beneath the frozen depths are whispers of lore...

Ahnah's world is shattered when her son is abducted by a creature from her grandmother's haunting tales — the Qalupalik. Fueled by love and unyielding courage, she plunges into a perilous realm where myths and legends come alive. Just when hope seems lost, her son is returned by someone she believed was gone forever—her first love. Now, faced with the pain of the past and the spark of rekindled romance, Ahnah must join forces with him and a powerful sea goddess. Together, they embark on a daring quest to destroy the Qalupalik and unravel an insidious plan that has already been set in motion.

This book is a sweet short story, with adventure, MERMAIDS and a little spice!
Sedna's Anchor is the first book in a series of urban

legend romances. Each book will be a standalone and can be read out of order. This book is my interpretation of two Inuit urban legends- the Qalupalik and Sedna the sea goddess.

Made in the USA
Middletown, DE
22 June 2025